It was the kind of kiss a man gives a woman he finds attractive.

Shane had only leaned over to kiss Kelly's cheek. But somehow the kiss went astray, landing on the corner of her mouth instead.

She felt her eyes widen, felt her breath lodge somewhere deep in her chest. Shane drew away only a fraction of an inch, his gaze locked with hers, a startled expression in his eyes. And then his mouth was on hers, and he was kissing her in a way he had never kissed her before.

Kelly's reaction was sheer pleasure. This, she thought dazedly, her hands settling tentatively on Shane's shoulders, was one amazing kiss....

Dear Reader,

This September, you may find yourself caught up in the hustle and bustle of a new school year. But as a sensational stress buster, we have an enticing fall lineup for you to pamper yourself with. Each month, we offer six brand-new romances about people just like you—trying to find the perfect balance between life, career, family and love.

For starters, check out *Their Other Mother* by Janis Reams Hudson—a feisty THAT SPECIAL WOMAN! butts head with a gorgeous, ornery father of three. This also marks the debut of this author's engaging new miniseries, WILDERS OF WYATT COUNTY.

Sherryl Woods continues her popular series AND BABY MAKES THREE: THE NEXT GENERATION with an entertaining story about a rodeo champ who becomes victim to his matchmaking daughter in *Suddenly, Annie's Father*. And for those of you who treasure stories about best-friends-turned-lovers, don't miss *That First Special Kiss* by Gina Wilkins, book two in her FAMILY FOUND: SONS AND DAUGHTERS series.

In *Celebrate the Child* by Amy Frazier, a military man becomes an integral part of his precious little girl's life—as well as that of her sweet-natured adopted mom. And when a secret agent takes on the role of daddy, he discovers the family of his dreams in Jane Toombs's *Designated Daddy*. Finally, watch for *A Cowboy's Code* by talented newcomer Alaina Starr, who spins a compelling love story set in the hard-driving West.

I hope you enjoy these six emotional romances created *by* women like you, *for* women like you!

Sincerely,

Karen Taylor Richman
Senior Editor

Please address questions and book requests to:
Silhouette Reader Service
U.S.: 3010 Walden Ave., P.O. Box 1325, Buffalo, NY 14269
Canadian: P.O. Box 609, Fort Erie, Ont. L2A 5X3

GINA WILKINS

THAT FIRST SPECIAL KISS

SPECIAL EDITION®

Published by Silhouette Books

America's Publisher of Contemporary Romance

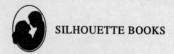 **SILHOUETTE BOOKS**

ISBN 0-373-24269-7

THAT FIRST SPECIAL KISS

Copyright © 1999 by Gina Wilkins

This edition published by arrangement with Harlequin Books S.A.

® and TM are trademarks of Harlequin Books S.A., used under license.
Trademarks indicated with ® are registered in the United States Patent
and Trademark Office, the Canadian Trade Marks Office and in other
countries.

Visit us at www.romance.net

Printed in U.S.A.

GINA WILKINS

declares that she is Southern by birth and by choice, and she has chosen to set many of her books in the South, where she finds a rich treasury of characters and settings. She particularly loves the Ozark mountain region of northern Arkansas and southern Missouri, and the proudly unique people who reside there. She and her husband, John, live in Arkansas, with their three children, Courtney, Kerry and David.

Chapter One

Kelly Morrison's tiny apartment almost reverberated with laughter, conversation and music. It was the first Saturday in November, and her group of single friends had gathered, as they did on the first weekend of each month, for an evening of gossip and games. They alternated homes, though not in any particular order, and tonight they had congregated at Kelly's place.

Carrying a tray of cheese cubes, fruit slices and crackers, she walked out of her kitchen with the slight limp she hardly even noticed anymore. She set the tray on the round oak table that took up one corner of her combination living room and dining room. Three men and two women were gathered around the table, waiting for her to rejoin them. "Whose turn is it?" she asked.

"Yours," Heather Pearson said, reaching for an apple slice. "Roll the dice."

Kelly took her seat, rolled the dice and moved her

game piece the required number of spaces. She groaned when she saw the category. "Sports…great. My worst category. Okay, what's the question?"

Heather's twin brother, Scott, read from a game card. "Who won the NASCAR Winston Cup series in 1995, 1997 and again in 1998, becoming the youngest driver ever to win three Winston Cup titles?"

Kelly mentally debated between the few race car drivers she could actually name. "Jeff Gordon?" she hazarded.

Scott nodded. "Correct."

From across the table, Michael Chang sighed gustily. "Man, she gets all the easy ones," he complained. "Who *didn't* know that one? My last question was about some obscure European playwright no one could have named except maybe his mother."

Kelly laughed and reached for her diet soda. "Just lucky, I guess."

She smiled at the friends gathered in mismatched chairs around her table: Scott Pearson, Michael Chang, Cameron North, Heather Pearson and Amber Wallace, all in their mid- to late-twenties. At twenty-four, Kelly was the youngest by a year or two, but she fit in very well.

It had always been very important to Kelly to fit in.

She looked automatically toward the empty folding chair next to her. Someone was absent from the gathering tonight, and she missed him—just as she would miss any of her friends who hadn't been able to attend the monthly event, she assured herself.

Following her glance, Heather mused, "Where do you suppose Shane is tonight? It's not like him to miss without calling."

"He didn't even call *you,* Cam?" Amber asked.

Brushing his heavy blond hair away from decidedly wicked blue eyes, Cameron lounged in his chair and shook his head. "Haven't heard from him today. I guess he got a, uh, better offer this evening."

Kelly frowned, reluctantly picturing Shane with the leggy, busty redhead he'd introduced her to at a party a couple of weeks earlier. Kelly hadn't liked her. At all. Of course it wasn't any of her business who Shane Walker dated, she thought hastily. She and Shane were buddies. Pals. Practically family. They made it a point not to get involved in each other's love lives.

Not that Kelly actually *had* a love life.

Scott was frowning at an empty plate. "Aren't there any more of those chocolate things?"

"You ate them all," his twin sister pointed out. "You pig. Some of the rest of us might've liked to have a few."

Kelly chuckled and pushed herself out of the chair again. "As it happens, there are more in the kitchen. Since I know how Scott is about chocolate, I bought extra."

Scott's green eyes lit with greed. "There are more?"

"Keep your paws off them, pal," Michael grumbled. "I haven't had any yet."

"Whose turn is it anyway?" Amber complained. "Isn't anyone paying attention to the game?"

Grinning, Kelly was halfway to the kitchen when her doorbell rang. She immediately altered her course. "I'll get it."

She threw open the door without bothering to check the peephole. And then she felt herself relax. Now the evening was complete.

A lanky cowboy stood on the walkway outside her ground-level apartment. He wore a denim jacket, jeans and an oatmeal-colored denim shirt with dusty boots and a worn leather belt. In deference to a light, misty rain that had been falling most of the day, a battered black Stetson was gripped in his left hand, which hung loosely at his side. His coffee-brown hair hung in a shaggy forelock over blue eyes that usually gleamed with amusement. Kelly saw no amusement there now.

"You look like you've had a rough day," she blurted impulsively.

Shane Walker grimaced and stepped across the threshold. "A guy always likes to be greeted with compliments."

She smiled apologetically. "It wasn't a criticism. Just a comment."

He smiled then, sexy dimples flashing. "Forget it. You're probably right. I've had a hell of a day. By the way, I know I promised I'd have your VCR back by tonight, but it's not ready yet. I haven't had time to take it apart and find out what's wrong with it."

"I'm in no hurry for it," she assured him. "Whenever you have time to look at it is fine with me. It was nice of you to volunteer to fix it, since I didn't really want to pay a repair bill for something I don't use that often anyway."

"I still think it'll be something minor, once I get a chance to work on it."

"Take your time. Go on over to the table and sit down. I'll get you something cold to drink."

He slung an arm around her shoulders and gave her a casual hug. "Thanks. I'd appreciate it."

As often as Shane had hugged her during the year and a half or so they'd known each other—and, since he was an affectionate and demonstrative person, there had been many friendly hugs—Kelly had never quite become ac-

customed to it. She always reacted with a quick jump of
pulse that she hid with a breezy smile and a brusque,
sisterly manner. She did so again now.

"Sit," she said, giving him a teasing push that served
to break the contact between them. "I'll be right back."

Shane sauntered toward the table, where he was
greeted warmly and noisily. By the time Kelly returned
with a cold soda for Shane and another plate of chocolate
cookies, he was already settled comfortably in his chair
and engaged in conversation with his friends. He
brushed off questions about his tardiness, saying only
that he'd been detained at the cattle ranch he owned and
operated with his father.

Amber pushed the game board away in exasperation
when no one showed any interest in reaching for the
dice. "I take it the game's over. Oh, well, I was losing
anyway."

"You always lose," Cameron drawled. "You just always seem to think it will be different next time."

Amber punched his arm, then giggled and sat on his
knee. She and Cameron had been dating for the past
three months—which, Kelly thought wryly, was pretty
much a record for Cameron. The whole gang had predicted disaster when the two long-time friends had become lovers—especially since everyone believed Amber
was more intensely involved than Cameron—but so far,
so good.

Kelly took her seat next to Shane. "How's the family?"

"Everyone's fine. Molly won a school poster contest
today. The prize was a fifty-dollar gift certificate. When
I left, she was poring over a catalog, trying to decide
what to buy."

Kelly smiled as she pictured Shane's twelve-year-old

half sister, a red-haired bundle of energy who brought a great deal of joy to her family, and whom Shane simply adored. "Good for her. What sort of poster did she make?"

"It was a contest sponsored by MADD—Mothers Against Drunk Driving. Molly's poster had an anti-alcohol slogan, and a picture she drew to illustrate it. I'm sure she'll want to show it to you next time you visit the ranch."

"I'll look forward to it." She studied him more closely, noting that his smile still didn't reach his eyes. He looked bone-tired, and maybe a little down. She didn't remember seeing him look quite this way before.

She wished she could think of something she could say to cheer him up.

Kelly was very fond of Shane—just as she was fond of all the friends she'd made during the year and a half that had passed since she and her best friend, Brynn Larkin, had moved to Dallas. Now Brynn was married to Dr. Joe D'Alessandro and had made a special place for herself among Joe's large, close-knit family. Brynn had also formed close bonds with the extended family of aunts, uncles and cousins she had discovered entirely by accident after moving to Dallas. Shane was one of Brynn's cousins.

Kelly and Brynn had considered themselves honorary sisters since they'd met in a foster home as young girls, when Brynn was fourteen and Kelly only eleven. Because of that connection, Kelly had been accepted among the Walker family with a warmth and generosity that had both astonished and delighted her. For the first time in longer than she could remember, she felt like a member of a family. And it meant more to her than she could ever put into words. Just as this group of friends had become very special to her because of the way they had taken her in when Shane had introduced her to them a little more than a year ago.

She wondered if she was the only one to suspect that something was bothering Shane. It would certainly be difficult for a casual observer to tell that there was anything wrong. He laughed at the others' jokes and told a few of his own. He jokingly fought Scott for the last chocolate cookie—and won. He teased Amber into a rosy blush, made an extravagant bet with Cameron over an upcoming football game, and talked airplanes with Michael, a professional charter pilot. Shane gave every appearance of being his usual, casually laid-back self.

And yet...

As if by accident, he glanced her way and caught her watching him. Their gazes held for a moment. Shane must have seen something in her expression. ''You okay?'' he asked, softly enough that none of the others could hear.

''I was going to ask the same of you,'' she admitted as quietly. ''Is anything wrong?''

He hesitated, glanced at the others, who were paying them no attention, then shrugged. ''I'll tell you later.''

Again Shane hid whatever he was feeling behind a quick quip and a lazy grin as he rejoined the conversation among the others. Kelly had always marveled at his ability to mask his emotions. His perpetual cheerfulness and exuberance made him very popular to nearly everyone who knew him, but she wondered how many people actually knew him well. She had always believed that there were parts of him he kept hidden—maybe even from those who were closest to him.

Or maybe, she thought ruefully, she was delusional. Maybe she was imagining depths to Shane that weren't there at all. Maybe he was exactly what he seemed—a happy-go-lucky, serenely untroubled young cowboy, perfectly content with his life. Maybe she simply wanted to believe she could sense things about Shane that no one else could. Which was ridiculous. She certainly didn't know Shane Walker better than his close-knit, loving family. Or this group of friends he'd known much longer than he'd known her.

"Kelly, are there any more of those chocolate things in the kitchen?" Scott—one of Shane's friends since adolescence—asked hopefully.

She smiled and shook her head. "Sorry, that was the last of them."

He sighed gustily. "Then I might as well go home."

"You aren't leaving yet?" Heather demanded. "It's barely eleven o'clock."

Scott cleared his throat. "I, er, have to look over some paperwork from the office."

"Bull," his twin retorted inelegantly. "You're going to Paula's place, aren't you?"

"And what if I am?" Scott asked defensively.

Heather rolled her eyes. "Tell him, guys. She's entirely wrong for him and everyone knows it but Scott."

Michael Chang immediately tried to change the subject. "Did anyone catch the score of the A & M game this afternoon?"

His effort backfired when Heather immediately rounded on him. "Michael, you've met Paula. Tell Scott what you think of her."

"I—uh—" Michael tugged at the collar of his knit shirt. "I thought she had several truly amazing features."

Cameron laughed. Amber punched his shoulder.

Heather turned to Shane. "He'll listen to you, Shane.

Tell Scott why I don't like it that he's spending so much time with Paula. Tell him how awful she is.''

Stretching back in his chair, Shane folded his hands over his flat stomach and tilted one corner of his mouth into a half smile. "You should know by now that I never get involved in anyone else's love life. If Scott enjoys spending time with Paula, I'd say that's his business, not mine."

Heather exhaled impatiently. "You guys are a lot of help. What about you, Kelly? Are you going to keep quiet, too?''

Cameron spoke before Kelly had a chance. "Kelly never gives advice. She's much too cautious."

Somewhat surprised by the assessment, since she'd never thought Cameron gave her much consideration, Kelly asked, "What makes you say that?"

"I'm an observer, remember?" the newspaper reporter drawled. "I watch people. You don't like making waves, and you hate it when anyone is mad at you. Giving advice involves taking a risk of being wrong—which, in turn, almost guarantees that someone will be upset with you. So—you keep your opinions to yourself, for the most part."

"Well, I..."

Grinning again, Cameron winked at her. "Don't try to deny it, kid. If you were the type to give personal advice, you'd have joined the others in warning Amber away from me."

Several throats were cleared in unison. Amber smiled a bit sappily at her lover. "I wouldn't have listened to Kelly any more than I listened to the others. I know you and I are meant to be together."

For only a moment, Kelly saw a somber expression cross Cameron's wickedly handsome face. And it occurred to her that if she *were* the type to offer advice to her friends, she would be more likely to warn Amber not to invest too much hope in a future with Cameron, than to suggest to Scott that Paula wasn't right for him. For one thing, she suspected that Scott, a twenty-eight-year-old attorney, was under no illusions about the avaricious and rather demanding woman he had been casually dating. She thought Heather's fears that Scott was getting too deeply involved were unfounded.

Scott pushed his chair away from the table. "I've gotta go. Heather, you can lecture me over lunch tomorrow at Mom's."

His twin muttered a disgruntled response, but returned his casual good-night kiss with an affection she made no effort to hide.

Scott's departure signaled an end to the evening. Heather left not long afterward, followed by Michael, Cameron and Amber, all of them pausing on their way out to thank Kelly for hosting them.

"Are we still going fishing next weekend, Shane?" Cameron asked from the threshold.

"Yeah, sure. I'll call you to set up the time."

"Great."

Amber pouted. "I still don't know why I can't go with you guys. I like to fish."

Cameron pulled playfully at a strand of Amber's dark hair. "Guys only. No girls allowed."

She was still arguing when Shane closed the door behind them.

Shane turned to Kelly with an ironic smile. "You suppose she doesn't know Cam wants to go fishing just to get away from her for a couple of hours?"

Kelly sighed. "You think so, too?"

"Yeah. She's starting to smother him. I suppose if

either of us was the type to give advice, we would tell her so.''

Smiling wryly, Kelly shook her head. ''I don't know about you, but I'm staying out of it.''

''So am I. I just hope it will end amicably rather than in a flaming disaster.''

So Shane, too, thought the romance between their friends was ill-fated. Like him, Kelly hoped the end of the affair wouldn't mean an end to a long friendship. But realistically, she couldn't see any other outcome.

She noticed then that Shane didn't seem to be in any hurry to leave. ''Would you like another soda?''

''To be honest, I'd rather have a cup of coffee—unless you're tired and ready for me to get lost.''

''Don't be ridiculous. You know you're always welcome here.'' She waved him toward the couch. ''Sit down. I'll get the coffee.''

He didn't hesitate. He was comfortably settled on the couch before Kelly had even made it to the kitchen doorway.

She wasn't gone long. She returned carrying a cup of coffee for him and a glass of water for herself. Shane patted the couch beside him as he reached for his coffee. ''Sit. You've been jumping up and down all evening being the gracious hostess.''

She sank onto the cushions beside him, took a sip of water and then set her glass on the low table in front of them. ''I didn't mind. I always enjoy having everyone over.''

''I notice you're limping quite a bit this evening. Is your leg bothering you?''

His matter-of-fact tone kept her from being self-conscious about the limp, a result of the serious car accident she was involved in a year and a half earlier. She had been lying in a hospital bed recuperating from that accident the first time she'd met Shane. He had seen her at her most vulnerable point and had watched her grow stronger since. During that time he had become one of her closest friends. "I'm fine. Just a little tired."

"Want me to massage it for you?"

Just the thought of having Shane massage her leg almost made her squirm on the couch, no matter how casually he'd suggested it. "No," she said a bit too quickly. "But, er, thanks for the offer."

"Sure." He sipped his coffee for a few moments, looking across the room toward nothing in particular. His thoughts seemed to be suddenly far away, and she suspected he was thinking again about whatever had bothered him earlier. She waited, knowing he would tell her when he was ready—if at all.

And then he cleared his throat. "My mother died Thursday. I found out this morning."

She didn't know what to say in response to his quiet announcement. Though she had become well acquainted with Shane's father, stepmother and young half sister, she had heard very little about his biological mother. She had been told that his mother was an alcoholic and that Shane had been so unhappy in her custody after his parents' divorce that he had run away from home when he was only twelve. He had somehow survived on the streets of Memphis, Tennessee, for two weeks before his distraught father had found him. Shane had never lived with his mother again after that. Kelly wasn't sure he had even seen her since.

Because she didn't know how he would respond to words of sympathy, she asked instead, "How did you find out?"

"Her sister called Dad and asked him to tell me. I

didn't mention it to the others tonight because I didn't want to talk about it then, but I wanted you to know.''

She was touched. She only wished she knew what to say. "I could tell something was upsetting you earlier, but I didn't mean to pry.''

He smiled at her and laid his hand over hers, which rested on her knee. "You weren't prying. You were concerned—and I appreciate it.''

Kelly entwined her fingers with his, offering comfort she sensed he needed. "How do you feel now?''

"I don't know," he admitted after a moment. "A little sad, I guess. Her life was such a mess—such a waste. She was only forty-eight. She should have had many years ahead of her, but she ruined her health with her drinking.''

He hesitated another moment, then added, "And I guess I feel a little guilty.''

Startled, Kelly frowned. 'Why on earth would you feel guilty?''

"It's hard to explain. It's just that—well, I've had a good life with Dad and Cassie and Molly. We've had each other, and Dad's and Cassie's extended families. We've been happy at the ranch. My mother was never happy.''

Kelly tightened her fingers. "Shane, your mother made her own choices. I know little of your family history, but you told me once that your father tried very hard to help her with her alcoholism. You said she simply wasn't willing to give it up. She chose addiction over the sort of happiness you and your father found. It was a waste, and a very sad one—but you shouldn't feel guilty about choices that were made when you were just a child.''

Shane leaned against the back of the couch, his gaze

still unfocused as he concentrated on his somber thoughts. "I went to see her a couple of years ago—right after my twenty-fifth birthday."

"I didn't know."

He shook his head. "I didn't tell anyone but Dad and Cassie. It was something I hadn't wanted to do before, but I finally felt compelled to make an effort. I still had so much anger against her, so much resentment—and I thought it was time to let it go. I thought there might even be a chance that I could help her."

Kelly could tell by Shane's voice that the reunion hadn't gone well. "The meeting didn't work out as you had hoped."

It hadn't been a question, but he answered it anyway, with a shake of his head. "She made it very clear that she hadn't thought of me as her son since I left her to live with my father. She said I was just like him—and she didn't want either of us trying to interfere in her life. And then she poured herself a drink and asked me to leave."

"I'm sorry." The words were inadequate, but the only ones she had.

He shrugged. "She didn't realize it, but she gave me one very high compliment. She said I was just like my dad."

Kelly had always been a bit envious of the intensely close relationship between Shane and his father. She hadn't seen her own career air force father in years. Perhaps that was one of the reasons she'd always felt close to Shane—she knew what it was like to be rejected by a parent. But at least Shane had his father. Kelly's mother had died when Kelly was a young girl, leaving her to be raised in a foster home.

As if suddenly aware of how much he'd revealed to

her, Shane sat up straight and cleared his expression, one corner of his mouth lifting into his usual indolent smile. ''Thanks for the coffee and sympathy, but I'd better go. It's late.''

Oddly reluctant to break the rare moment of intimacy, she forced herself to smile. ''Both the coffee and the sympathy are available whenever you need them.''

Still holding her hand, he stood and pulled her to her feet. ''You're a good friend, Kelly Morrison.''

Her reaction to his words was inexplicably bitter-sweet, but the smile she gave him was genuine. ''You've been a good friend to me, too, Shane Walker.''

''Walk me to the door?'' he asked, tucking her hand beneath his arm.

Privately relishing the feel of work-hardened muscles beneath the fabric of his sleeve, she matched her steps to his as they crossed the small room. Shane stopped at the curvy oak coat rack beside the door to retrieve his jacket and hat. She watched as he donned his jacket, and then she asked, ''Will there be a funeral for your mother?''

He shook his head. ''Her sister arranged a private cremation. It was all over before she even called Dad. There was no estate to settle, so there's nothing for Dad or me to do now.''

He seemed to have shaken off the hint of depression she'd noticed earlier, replacing it with a stoic acceptance of his mother's sad fate. Kelly hoped it had helped him just to talk about his feelings to someone who cared about him, and who could understand his mixed emotions about a long-absent parent.

''Good night, Shane. Drive carefully.''

His answering smile was unshadowed now, even a bit

teasing as he responded to her rather maternal admonition. "I'll do my best."

She opened the door.

Shane started to cross the threshold, but then he paused and turned to her again. "Um, Kelly—thanks for letting me talk it out, okay?"

"You're welcome."

On an impulse, she reached out to hug him. His arms closed warmly around her, his cheek resting against her short, blond hair. For several long moments, they stood entwined in the open doorway, oblivious to the cool night air wafting in from outside. Kelly offered comfort in the embrace and Shane accepted it. It was a hug between friends who had hugged many times before.

And then something changed. She became suddenly aware of how warm he was against her. How firmly he held her against his lean, solid body. She felt his breath against her cheek, and noted the appealing scents of soap and spicy aftershave. Something buried deeply inside her responded to those observations, quivering to life.

And in reaction, Kelly pulled away, her action so swift and abrupt that Shane nearly stumbled. His eyebrows rose quizzically as he studied her flushed face. "What was *that?*" he asked humorously.

"That," she replied, her voice crisp, "was me telling you it's time to go home. You're wearing a jacket, but I'm freezing."

It was a lie, of course. She was more in danger of burning than freezing. And she reacted to that danger with a very logical retreat. She all but pushed him out the door. "Good night, Shane."

"Good night, Kel—"

She closed the door in his face, then sagged against it. *Friends,* she reminded herself. She and Shane were friends. Almost family. And she would do nothing to jeopardize that precious relationship.

Chapter Two

Shane spent Sunday afternoon with his father, restringing barbed wire fencing at the back section of the small, but sufficiently profitable cattle ranch they owned and operated together. It was hard work, but a nice day—cool, crisp, clear—and Shane enjoyed being outside. November signaled the beginning of the slow time for their ranch. Calves had been weaned and sold, the herd had been culled and vaccinated, the haying was finished and preparations had been made for winter feeding. Calving would start in mid-January, but until then they had some time to catch up on paperwork and general maintenance.

Shane and Jared didn't talk much while they worked. They had always been comfortable with long stretches of companionable silence, feeling no need to make small talk just to fill in the spaces. Jared was the one who spoke first after a long, busy pause. "How are you doing, son?"

Just as they didn't need small talk, they rarely had to elaborate for each other. Shane knew exactly what his father referred to. "I'm fine, Dad. You?"

Jared lifted one broad shoulder. "Yeah."

The single syllable spoke volumes as far as Shane was concerned. Like his son, Jared was saddened by the meaningless, early end to a wasted life, but he had long since resigned himself to his ex-wife's determination to self-destruct, and his own inability to stop her. Jared had gone on with his life, but he hadn't forgotten the woman who had borne his first child.

Glancing over his shoulder, Jared studied Shane's face for a moment. "You seem to be in better spirits today than you were yesterday."

Shane grunted as he put his muscles into stretching the wire taut. He fastened the wire and straightened. "I feel better about it. Kelly and I talked awhile last night and I guess I needed that."

He had needed it more than he'd realized, actually. He'd been so troubled by his mother's meaningless death that he almost hadn't gone to Kelly's at all. And then something had drawn him there. He'd known as soon as she opened the door, greeting him with a warm, pretty smile and a look of concern in her striking emerald eyes, that he'd made the right decision.

"You and Kelly seem to be getting pretty tight lately."

A bit surprised by his father's comment, Shane looked up from his work. "Kelly and I have been friends since we met. Nothing has changed."

"Hmm."

Frowning, he searched his father's weathered face. "What's that supposed to mean?"

Jared deftly twisted wire around a steel post to fasten a strand of barbed wire in place. "What?"

"The way you said 'hmm.' Like there was something else you wanted to say."

"I don't know what you're talking about. I just said 'hmm.'"

Shane felt a need, for some reason, to continue to justify his personal discussion with Kelly. "Kelly's practically a member of the family. It isn't unusual that she and I would talk about family matters."

"Because they were raised in the same foster home, Kelly and your cousin Brynn are sisters at heart, not in fact. We all consider Kelly part of the family, but there is, of course, no blood relationship."

Shane had never heard Jared make that distinction before, and he wondered why he did so now. "So are you saying I *shouldn't* have talked to Kelly?"

"Of course not." Jared sounded almost irritated by the question. "I just said 'hmm,' Shane. Why are you making so much out of it?"

He couldn't answer, other than that he was baffled by his father's uncharacteristically cryptic conversation. Jared usually stated his thoughts bluntly and without prevarication. But if he was trying to make a particular point this afternoon, it eluded Shane completely.

Jared changed the subject before Shane could decide what to say. "Cassie's picking up the tickets tomorrow for our vacation next month. You're still okay with watching Molly for ten days?"

Deciding with some relief to follow his father's conversational lead, Shane hefted the remaining roll of barbed wire into the back of Jared's pickup. "I'm looking forward to it. Molly and I will have a great time."

"Yeah, well, you've never had her for more than a

week before. I hope you know what you're getting your-self into.''

Shane chuckled. He was unashamedly crazy about his twelve-year-old half sister. He hadn't even hesitated to let her stay at his house while Jared and Cassie took a long overdue vacation after Thanksgiving. He was con-vinced it was the best arrangement for everyone. His house was on the ranch, within sight of the larger, main house Molly shared with her parents. She could catch the school bus at the usual spot by the ranch's entrance gate. And she would be around to take care of the me-nagerie of pets she had accumulated during the past few years.

"No sweat," he said with certainty. "I can handle it."

"Hmm."

Those enigmatic "hmms" were beginning to get on his nerves. He gathered the remainder of their tools, threw them into the truck, then stripped off his work gloves. "Didn't Cassie say something about frying chicken for dinner?"

Jared glanced at his watch. "By the time we finish at the barn and get cleaned up, she'll probably have dinner ready for us."

"Sounds great. Let's go."

They climbed into the truck, Jared behind the wheel. During the short, bumpy ride back to the barn, Shane found himself thinking of Kelly again and wondering why Jared had seemed so ambivalent toward her today. Jared had always seemed fond of Kelly, as Shane was, himself. Was he only imagining that Jared acted now as if something had changed? And, if so, what could it be?

A white delivery van pulled up in front of Shane's white-frame bungalow late the next afternoon. Shane was just walking up to the house after working in the barn, and he was grimy and sweaty. He had planned on heading straight for the shower. The sight of the van pulling to a stop in his driveway made him pause.

He spoke to the black-and-white border collie at his heels, who had gone on alert at the sight of a stranger in the driveway. "Chill out, Paulie."

In response to the familiar command, the dog relaxed and began to wag its tail.

"Can I help you?" Shane asked the young man who climbed out of the driver's door of the van.

"Are you Shane Walker?"

"Yes."

The delivery driver nodded. "Got something for you."

Shane was startled when the driver pulled an arrangement of cut flowers out of the van. Only then did he notice the sign painted on the side of the vehicle—Francine's Flowers And Gifts. The driver dumped the large arrangement unceremoniously into Shane's dirty hands. "Enjoy," he said.

Shane gaped at the multicolored blooms arranged in a clear glass vase. "You're—uh—sure these are for *me?*"

"Says Shane Walker on the tag. This address." The young man winked. "If some woman sent *me* flowers, I'd say she was giving me a pretty clear message."

Balancing the vase in his left arm, Shane dug into his jeans pocket and pulled out a five—the only cash he had with him at the moment. "Er—thanks," he said, offering the bill to the delivery driver and hoping he had the etiquette right. He'd never been the recipient of flowers before.

The driver cheerfully pocketed the money and climbed back into his van. A minute later, Shane was standing alone outside his house, the scents of carnations, mums and other blooms wafting around him. Curious, he carried the arrangement inside and set it on a table. The fall colors matched the rusts and creams he and Cassie had selected when he'd decorated his cozy cottage.

He plucked a card from deep within the bouquet. He hoped it hadn't been Gayla who'd sent them. He'd taken the curvy redhead out a time or two, but had backed off when she'd seemed to make more of his asking her out than he had intended. Flowers from her at this point would certainly be awkward, since that would be a sign that she hadn't taken his hint about their future together—or lack of one.

But it hadn't been Gayla who'd sent the arrangement, he saw at once. Printed in flowery, engraved script at the top of the small cardboard rectangle was the message, "Thinking of you." Written below in a familiar scrawl were two simple words, "Love, Kelly."

Shane was both touched and bemused by her gesture. She had sent the flowers because his mother had died. Coming from Kelly, the flowers seemed more than the standard expression of sympathy. The gesture was a sign of empathy, which, under the circumstances, meant even more to him.

On an impulse, he leaned over to sniff a golden bloom. The scent reminded him of the faintly floral fragrance Kelly often wore. He'd always liked it.

He glanced at his watch, wondering if she was home yet. If he remembered correctly, she was usually home early on Monday afternoons. Kelly was a full-time graduate student at the University of Texas at Dallas, her tuition paid by scholarships, her living expenses met by her part-time work with a local children's speech and hearing treatment center. He knew money was a bit tight for her, yet she'd sent him flowers to let him know he was in her thoughts. He was touched by her generosity.

Her phone rang only twice before she answered. "Hello?"

"No one ever sent me flowers before," he said without bothering to identify himself.

There was a hint of a smile in her voice when she answered. "You mean I'm your first?"

He chuckled, pleased that the conversation had begun with their usual easy humor. "Yeah. And you know what they say...you never forget your first."

"Good. I wouldn't want you to forget me."

He couldn't imagine that ever happening. He couldn't even picture his life without Kelly in it now. After all, he reminded himself quickly, Kelly was part of the family. Just like a cousin to him. Sort of.

"I called to thank you," he said a bit more seriously. "That was a really nice thing to do."

"My favorite teacher sent me flowers when my mother died. I've never forgotten how it brought me peace to look at the beautiful flowers in the days after the funeral. I kept them until they were nothing more than dry sticks. I still have one bloom that I pressed in a heavy book. Maybe it was kind of dippy, but when I thought of you today, I remembered those flowers that meant so much to me and...well, I thought you might like some, too."

"It wasn't dippy," Shane assured her, gazing at the colorful blossoms. "It was...nice."

Nice. A fairly tepid word to describe Kelly's generous

and thoughtful gesture, but it was the best Shane could come up with at the moment.

"I'm glad you like them." Seeming to grow uncomfortable with the subject, Kelly abruptly changed it. "How's your family?"

"Everyone's fine. You haven't been out to the ranch in a while, have you?"

"No. Between school and work, it's hard to find free time. I was particularly sorry to miss Molly's birthday party last week, but I had to work."

"Molly loved the gift you sent. But she would have liked you to be here, of course. And Sunny misses you," he commented, referring to the horse Kelly often rode when she visited.

"I miss her, too. I look forward to coming for Thanksgiving. I'm so glad your parents invited me."

"Of course they invited you. You're part of the family, Kelly." He changed the subject abruptly. "Are you planning to go to Nancy's birthday party for Jackie O'Brien Thursday night? Do you need a ride—or, uh, do you have a date?"

"No, I can't go. I have an exam Friday. I have to study Thursday night."

"Dumb night for a party for working folks, huh?"

Kelly laughed. "You going to say that to Nancy?"

"No way," he replied, feigning fear. "She'd take my head off. Nancy does not take well to criticism."

"True. But she throws great parties. And Thursday is Jackie's thirtieth birthday. Are you taking a date?" she asked very casually.

"No. I'll probably just drop in during the evening, if I've got time." It had been quite a while since he had a date, actually—if he didn't count Gayla. Which he didn't, since there had never been any real chemistry between them. He'd only kissed her a time or two, and had found no desire within himself to take it any further.

He guessed he'd just been too busy and too absorbed with the operation of the ranch to even think about getting involved with anyone.

"Well, have fun. Think of me slaving over my books while you're partying at Nancy's."

He chuckled. "My heart bleeds for you. Would you rather be doing what I did this afternoon—shoveling manure out of barn stalls?"

"I, uh, think I'd rather study, thanks."

"Yeah, that's what I thought. And speaking of my afternoon's exertions, I guess I'd better shower before dinner."

"Good idea."

"Thanks again for the flowers."

"You're welcome again. Goodbye, Shane."

He didn't say goodbye in return. He didn't really like that word—especially when it came to people he cared about. Like Kelly—who, he reminded himself as he smelled the flowers one more time, was just like a member of his family.

Thursday night found Kelly exactly where she had predicted she would be—alone in her apartment with a stack of books and a can of diet soda. She didn't usually mind studying, since she enjoyed attending classes and had only a little more than a semester remaining to earn her master's degree. But for some reason, she had found it difficult to concentrate on her books this evening.

She couldn't help thinking about the party she was missing. It wasn't that she was the type who could never miss a party. And she was only marginally acquainted with Jackie, in whose honor the party was being given.

It was actually fairly rare that Kelly accepted party invitations, since she didn't usually have much time to spare. But tonight she wondered who'd made it to Nancy's party. Were Cameron and Amber there, still going strong in their new relationship? Had Michael Chang, who'd been undecided the last time she'd talked to him, decided to go? Had Shane found time to "drop by," as he'd said he might do?

It wasn't hard to picture her friends laughing and having a great time at Nancy's. Food and conversation would be plentiful, and the big-screen TV would be tuned in to the sports channel. If Shane was there, he would be working the room, making the guys laugh with his endless supply of jokes, charming the women with his easy flirting.

Shane was very good at parties. Kelly usually enjoyed them herself—except for those times when she suffered from old insecurities about not fitting in. Being an outsider. She would occasionally find herself suddenly battling shyness, uncertain what to say or do. Fortunately those episodes were rare, and had grown even more uncommon during the past year, since she had carved such a comfortable niche for herself in Dallas.

Like her little apartment, she thought, glancing up from her books to look around her cozy nest in approval. She'd decorated sparingly, a choice due more to finances than taste, but every item had been selected because she liked it. She had utilized warm, rich colors and comfortable textures, enlarging small spaces with artfully placed mirrors, brightening dark corners with lamps and candles. This was home for her now, and she was happy here—despite the occasional lonely evenings. Like this one.

She nearly jumped out of her seat when her doorbell

rang at just after nine o'clock that evening. She couldn't imagine who was calling on her at this hour on a Thursday night. She realized she'd been sitting in one place too long when her permanently weakened right leg protested her quick rise from her chair. She shook it a little as she moved to the door, trying to loosen the stiff muscles. Straightening the oversize electric-blue sweater she wore with black leggings and black ballet slippers, she checked the peephole, then broke into a smile when she recognized the man making faces at her through the viewer.

"Shane," she said, throwing open the door. "What are you doing here?"

Certain of his welcome, he sauntered in without waiting for an invitation. Kelly gave him a quick once-over as he passed her, noting that he had swapped his usual uniform of denim shirt, jeans and boots for a long-sleeve, dark red polo shirt with loose-fitting khakis and brown suede oxfords. Shane Walker was one fine-looking man, and Kelly was honest enough with herself to admit she found him attractive, even if she had no intention of ever risking their friendship by acting on that attraction.

He was carrying a large paper bag in his right hand. He set it on the table next to her stack of textbooks. "How's the studying going? Ready for the big test?"

"I think so. I was just about to put the books away for the evening."

"Great." Shane rubbed his hands together in satisfaction. "Then the party can begin."

She lifted her eyebrows. "Party?"

With what she had always secretly labeled his "evil child grin," Shane sauntered over to her stereo, tuned in a top-forty station, then returned to open the bag he'd carried in. "Since you couldn't come to the party, I brought the party to you," he announced.

He pulled out a shiny silver-and-purple, cone-shaped party hat and plopped it on her head, sliding the elastic band under her chin to hold it in place. "It's you," he proclaimed, then solemnly settled a green-and-gold cardboard top hat on his own dark head.

Reaching up to straighten her hat, Kelly couldn't help giggling. "You really are insane."

"I've just gotten started." He dove into the bag again and pulled out a bottle of wine and two plastic wineglasses. The bottle had been opened, but most of the wine still remained, Kelly noted. Shane filled both glasses, then gave one to Kelly. "To Jackie," he said, lifting his glass.

She repeated the toast to the birthday girl, then took a sip. And promptly choked. "What *is* that?"

His own drink untasted, Shane made a production of checking the bottle label. *"Château de Bubba,"* he pretended to read aloud. "Bottled last week in Alamogordo."

"Let me guess. Chuck the Cheapskate brought wine for the party."

"Good guess. Everyone insisted that I should bring some to you."

Taking another cautious sip, Kelly barely repressed a shudder. "I'll have to find a way to thank them all."

Without touching his own glass, Shane reached into the bag again. Two covered foam containers revealed sizable portions of birthday cake, each piece bearing several pink icing flowers. With the flair of a stage magician, he produced two birthday candles, which he stuck into the slices and lit with a lighter also pulled from the bag.

"We have to sing 'Happy Birthday' to Jackie now," he instructed gravely. He started the song in a deliberately off-key warble. Kelly alternately giggled and sang along, then followed his example and blew out the candle on her cake. A thin stream of smoke tickled her nose, making her giggle again.

"Is there anything else in that bag?" she asked after he produced plastic forks.

"But of course," he replied. The next item he brought out was a small, brightly wrapped gift. "Can't have a birthday party without presents."

"But Jackie isn't here to open it."

"This one isn't for Jackie. This is for you." Shane pressed the box into her hand.

"For me? But it isn't my birthday."

"It's an unbirthday present," he informed her. "Go ahead. Open it."

Shaking her head in amused exasperation at his unpredictability, Kelly tore off the wrapping paper and opened the box inside. And then smiled in delight. "A toothpick holder. Shane, it's lovely."

The delicate cut-glass cylinder narrowed from a wide, fluted opening to a small, flat bottom. It was a perfect specimen, without a chip or scratch that she could see at first glance. It would make a very nice addition to the small collection of antique toothpick holders she'd whimsically begun a few years earlier. "Where did you find it?"

"Cassie and Molly found a dresser for Molly's bedroom at an antique store in Fort Worth. I took them in my truck to pick it up yesterday, and I spotted this while Cassie was paying for the dresser. I thought you might like to add it to your collection. The salesclerk said it's a nice example from the early 1940s."

"I love it. Thank you." She carried the little container to the glass-fronted cabinet in which she kept her few dishes and the six other toothpick holders that made up her entire collection. She set it beside her most valuable piece, a delicate urn-shaped holder rimmed with fourteen-karat gold, a gift from Brynn last Christmas. This little gift from Shane was as precious to her as anything she owned.

Closing the cabinet door, she tilted her head to admire her newly expanded collection, then nearly choked when the elastic band beneath her chin tightened. She pulled the hat off as she turned, smiling at Shane. "Have I ever mentioned that you can be very sweet?"

He looked quickly around in exaggerated concern. "Hey, quiet! Someone might hear you. I've got a reputation to maintain."

"Too late," she said, unable to resist reaching out to pinch his dimpled cheek. "Everyone already knows what a sweetie you are."

And he looked so darned cute in that green-and-gold party hat, she couldn't help thinking as she laughed and pinched his cheek again.

Grinning, Shane caught her hand in his and pulled it away. "Stop. You're embarrassing me."

"All kidding aside, it really was sweet of you to buy a toothpick holder for my collection. And to bring the unbirthday party to me. Thank you."

He leaned over to brush a quick kiss against her cheek. "You're welcome." And then he straightened and motioned to the very small expanse of wooden floor between her dining and living areas. "Speaking of our unbirthday party, we've just gotten started. Dance with me."

A popular slow ballad had just begun to play on the

radio as he extended his hand to her. Kelly hesitated before placing her hand into his. There had been a time when she had loved to dance. But that was before the near-tragic car accident had damaged her legs and left her with an awkward limp. "I—uh—"

"We can't have a party without dancing." Shane tugged her gently into his arms. "Just one dance."

Giving in to his encouragement and her own temptation, she placed her right hand in his left and rested her other hand on his shoulder. "Just one dance," she agreed.

She had never danced with Shane before, she realized suddenly, vividly aware of how closely his cowboy-tough body moved against hers—pretty much a necessity since their dancing space was so limited. She hadn't danced since her accident, actually. Trust Shane to be the one to give her courage to try again.

Shane had been one of her most encouraging supporters ever since he'd met her while she was still lying in the hospital only days after her accident. He and his father, Jared, and Jared's extended family of siblings and in-laws had taken Kelly and Brynn under their wing after hearing about the accident they'd had the very day they'd moved to Dallas, leaving them without a place to stay or anyone to turn to during the early days of Kelly's recovery. It hadn't mattered that Brynn and Kelly were strangers to them then. They had been alone and in need, and the Walkers and D'Alessandros hadn't hesitated to come to their aid.

And then they had discovered by a stunning accident that Brynn was the daughter of one of the long-lost Walker brothers, who had died barely seven months before Brynn was born. He had left his unmarried and emotionally unstable young girlfriend to try to raise her child alone, unaware of the network of support she could have received had she known about Miles Walker's siblings. That Brynn had been brought back into the family years later was a miracle they all still marveled at, and which eldest sister, Layla Walker Samples, maintained was divine intervention rather than bizarre coincidence. After seeing how happy Brynn had been since finding her family and marrying Joe D'Alessandro, the handsome young doctor who had operated on Kelly's legs, Kelly had privately agreed with Layla. It must have taken more than happenstance to bring her and Brynn to this place at that particular time.

"You dance very well," Shane commented, smiling down at her in a way that would make her heart flutter, if she was susceptible to that sort of thing from him, she thought, ignoring the definite fluttering sensation in her chest.

"For a gimp?" she asked lightly, trying to hide her self-consciousness behind self-deprecating humor.

Shane didn't find it amusing. He frowned. "For anyone," he corrected. "You're very graceful and light on your feet. There's no reason you shouldn't dance any time you want to."

No reason except the faint, nagging ache that was already making itself known in her right knee, she thought ruefully. While she had regained much of her former agility, too much unaccustomed activity usually left her sore and stiff. She didn't complain, since she'd been lucky not to lose the leg entirely—the injuries had been almost that bad. But she couldn't help thinking sometimes of how blithely she'd once taken her physical fitness for granted.

Shane's hand rested at the small of her back. His fingers flexed. The slight movement sent a shiver through her, and made her aware once again of how very close they were. Close enough for her to feel the heat of him. Close enough for her to feel his breath against her temple. Close enough that she found herself wanting to be even closer.

She stumbled away from him just as the song ended. ''Thank you for the dance,'' she said. ''But shouldn't we eat our cake before it gets stale?''

Shane frowned a moment, then shoved his hands in his pockets. ''Sure, let's have our cake,'' he said, his voice revealing nothing of his thoughts. ''And you've hardly touched your wine.''

''Um—why don't I make coffee to go with the cake?'' she suggested quickly, glancing at the cheap wine with a not-so-subtle grimace.

''Coffee sounds much better,'' he agreed with a chuckle, and moved away from her to retrieve the pieces of cake.

Kelly felt herself relax as the distance between them increased a bit. As fond as she was of Shane, there was something that made her distinctly uncomfortable about being in his arms.

Chapter Three

By the time Kelly returned with steaming cups of coffee, Shane had settled onto the couch, the two slices of birthday cake waiting on the coffee table. As she set the cups on the table, Kelly was amused to see a paper plate holding two very large, chocolate-dipped strawberries. "More goodies from your bag, I take it?"

"Yeah. These were harder to smuggle out. Everyone got greedy with the strawberries. Strangely enough, no one complained when I took the bottle of wine."

"Imagine that."

Shane chuckled and picked up one of the strawberries. "These are great. Try one." He held the fruit to her lips.

Obligingly she opened her mouth to take a bite of the chocolate-dipped berry. And then she closed her eyes and moaned in appreciation of the mingled sweet and tart flavors. "Oh, that's heavenly," she murmured, then opened her eyes.

She found Shane closer than she'd expected, his face only inches from hers, his eyes focused on her mouth. He held the strawberry poised for her next bite. "More?" he asked, his voice a low rumble.

"More," she replied. But instead of letting him feed her another bite, she plucked the strawberry from his fingers and bit into it herself.

Shane drew back and picked up his plastic fork. "The cake is pretty good," he said after taking a bite.

Finishing the strawberry, Kelly set the stem aside, but didn't immediately reach for her cake or coffee. She wasn't ready to lose the tastes of rich chocolate and sweet strawberry. "Why did you leave the party?"

"Nancy overinvited—as usual—and I could hardly move at her place. Seemed like there was hardly enough air for everyone. I started thinking about how nice it would be to spend a quiet hour or so with you, so I took a chance you'd be finished with your studying, and here I am."

She twisted to face him, resting an elbow against the back of the couch and propping her cheek on her fist. "You usually like crowds."

"I guess I just wasn't in the mood tonight."

She studied him closely, wondering if he was still trying to deal with his mother's death. As if he'd read her thoughts, Shane smiled and patted her bent knee. "Stop fretting. I'm fine. Just a little tired. Dad's trying to get ready for his vacation with Cassie, and he's going to spend the next three weeks working like a demon—and working me right along with him. He hasn't taken a vacation in so long, he acts as if the whole place is in danger of crumbling to dust while he's gone."

She smiled. "I know Cassie's really looking forward

to getting away for a few days. How's Molly handling the thought of a whole ten days without her parents?''

Shane's answering smile was rueful. ''Actually, she seems to think it's going to be a blast. I think she's planning to be totally spoiled and pampered during that week.''

''And won't she be?''

He grinned. ''No doubt about it.''

''And you aren't worried about being responsible for a twelve-year-old girl for that long?''

''Why should I be? Molly and I are going to have a good time. She'll be in school during the days, and we have all kinds of great plans for the evenings. It'll be fun.''

Shane's unabashed devotion to his little sister was one of the many things Kelly admired about him. She wondered how many twenty-seven-year-old bachelors would be so eager to baby-sit an adolescent girl so his father and stepmother could take a much-needed vacation.

Shane finished his cake and coffee, then glanced at his watch. ''I'd better head for the ranch. You have your test tomorrow and you should get a good night's sleep.'' He broke into a smile. ''See? I know just what to say to Molly during the time she stays with me.''

Kelly nodded gravely. ''You sounded very paternal.''

''It's going to be a snap,'' he anticipated breezily.

''I'm sure you're right.'' But she was aware she didn't sound quite as confident as Shane. She knew a bit more than he did about the unpredictability of twelve-year-old girls.

He reached for the dishes. ''I'll help you clean up before I go.''

She put her hand over his, stopping him. ''Leave it. It'll only take me a few minutes to clear this away.''

He nodded and stood. "Well…good luck with your test."

"Thank you. I need all the luck I can get."

Shane usually kissed her cheek when he left. It was a long-standing habit, and she had never attached too much meaning to it, since he tended to be very generous with his hugs and kisses. She held the door for him, mentally bracing herself for that casually affectionate brush of his lips. Shane paused at the doorway, leaned toward her—then hesitated, his gaze on her mouth.

Her lips began to tingle as if she could already feel his mouth against hers. Odd, she thought with a swallow.

Shane gave her a slightly crooked smile and stepped away without touching her. "Good night, Kelly. I hope you ace your test."

Why *hadn't* he kissed her? Had he somehow sensed her mixed emotions about it? He wouldn't have thought twice about kissing his cousins, or his aunts, or even his friends, Heather or Amber. What made Kelly different, all of a sudden? "Thanks again for the toothpick holder."

He sketched her a funny little salute in lieu of a reply and stepped outside, closing the door behind him.

Staring at that unrevealing panel of wood, Kelly slowly shook her head. Sometimes it seemed that the more time she spent with Shane Walker, the less she really knew him.

"That dress looks fabulous on you, Kelly. You really should buy it."

Kelly looked away from the three-way mirror to smile at her longtime best friend, Brynn Larkin D'Alessandro. "You think so?"

"Absolutely." Brynn walked thoughtfully around her,

studying the close-fitting red dress. "It's perfect for you. And at sixty percent off, it's a fantastic price. You shouldn't pass it up."

Tempted, Kelly looked into the dressing room mirror again. The dress did fit very well, falling in a graceful line from double spaghetti straps to the floating just-above-the-knee hem. The crimson color looked good with her blond hair, gold-dusted complexion and dark green eyes. She hadn't come to the mall to buy a dress on this Saturday afternoon, but when she'd seen this one on a clearance rack, she'd been unable to resist trying it on.

She twisted to look at the back of her right arm, which was bared by the sleeveless garment. "What about the scar on this arm? Is it too noticeable? The scars on my legs I can conceal with glittery hose or something, but this one…"

"It's only a scar," Brynn said dismissively. "You look so pretty no one will notice that thin white line. I think you should get the dress."

"It *is* a bargain," Kelly admitted, glancing at the price tag again. "But I really don't know if I need it. Where would I wear it?"

"The holidays are coming up. Surely there will be a party or two you'll want to attend."

Kelly turned slowly in front of the mirror again, picturing the dress with the glittering costume jewelry she'd bought last year. It would look good at a holiday party, she thought, weakening further. And at sixty percent off, she could almost justify the expense.

But she really shouldn't buy it. She was trying to save a little extra money for Christmas gifts.

"Kelly! Hi, what's up?"

Kelly looked around to see Amber Wallace entering

the dressing room area, carrying a sizable stack of clothes to try on. "Hi, Amber. I see you and I both read the same sales ads."

Amber grinned. "Yeah. I need some new clothes, and I'm short on cash, so I hope there will be something that fits from the clearance rack."

"You remember my friend Brynn?"

"Of course." Amber smiled at Brynn. "How are you?"

"Fine, thank you," Brynn answered with the slightly shy courtesy that was so characteristic of her.

Amber looked back at Kelly, studying the red dress with obvious interest. "That's a great dress. Are you buying it?"

"I haven't decided," Kelly admitted. "I'm not sure I really need it..."

"If you don't want it, I'd like to try it on. You and I are about the same size. I think that dress would look good on me, don't you?"

Kelly was sure the red dress would look gorgeous on dark-haired, blue-eyed Amber. Maybe it would even look better on Amber than it did on Kelly herself. It was that somewhat-less-than-noble thought that made her clutch the dress more tightly around her and blurt out, "Sorry, but I think I will buy it. As Brynn just pointed out, I can wear it to holiday parties."

Amber looked disappointed, but resigned. "It does look good on you. Any particular guy you're trying to impress?"

"Of course not," Kelly answered quickly. "I'm buying it for myself."

"Oh." Amber cast one more rather wistful glance at the dress, then looked at the garments she held. "I just hope one of these looks as good on me. I *am* trying to impress someone in particular.''

Kelly didn't have to ask who. "How is Cameron?"

Amber's bright smile was dimmed only by the faint shadow in her eyes. "He's wonderful, of course. I wish I could have spent today with him, but he and Shane had that fishing trip planned. I don't know why they wouldn't let me go along. I love to fish. And Cameron didn't even want to do anything tonight. He said after getting up at dawn to go fishing, he'll just want to go home alone and crash tonight.''

Kelly and Brynn exchanged a quick, meaningful glance before Kelly looked back at Amber. "It's probably good for you and Cameron to spend a day apart every once in a while. He can do guy things with Shane and you can do your shopping and whatever. Why don't you come over to my place later? We can watch old movies and gossip about all our friends.''

Amber smiled a little, but shook her head. "Thanks, but I'm knitting a sweater for Cameron for Christmas. It's the hardest pattern I've ever tried and I've barely gotten started. I guess I'll stay home and work on that tonight.''

Kelly looked at Brynn again. Brynn shrugged slightly, as if to say Kelly had done all she could.

"I'm going to try these on now," Amber said, moving toward a dressing room. "Good to see you again, Brynn. I'll call you, okay, Kelly?"

"Sure. See ya, Amber.''

Kelly stepped into her own little nook and changed quickly back into the sweater and jeans she'd worn on her shopping trip. She paid for the red dress and then she and Brynn left the store and walked through the mall to a coffee bar. Only when they were settled in a booth behind steaming cups of cappuccino did Kelly mention Amber. "I'm really afraid she's going to be hurt."

Brynn nodded somberly. "She's rather desperately infatuated with him, isn't she?"

"*Desperate* is the word," Kelly agreed glumly. "She can't think of anything but Cameron these days. She's so obsessed with him that she practically has no other life—and she used to be so active and independent. I honestly don't know what's going to happen when it ends."

"You're so sure it *will* end?"

She sighed. "I wish I could say I thought there was a chance that they will be married and live happily ever after, but I really can't see it. Cameron just doesn't seem as committed to this relationship as Amber is."

"That's going to be awkward in your group of friends, isn't it? If Amber and Cameron have an unpleasant breakup, it's going to be difficult for them to continue seeing each other at your monthly get-togethers."

Kelly stared glumly into her cup. "It's going to be awful. Heather and I have been very close to Amber during the past year. And Shane, Scott and Cameron have been best friends for almost as long as any of them can remember. The divided loyalties alone will probably make our gatherings impossible."

"That would be such a shame. I hate to see anyone get hurt." Brynn glanced down at the rings on her left hand. "I would love to see everyone as happy as Joe and I have been."

If Kelly were the jealous type, she would certainly find it hard not to envy Brynn's good fortune during the past year and a half. Brynn had fallen in love with and married a gorgeous surgeon who simply adored her in return, and she had been immediately accepted into her husband's large, close-knit family. Finding her own family of aunts, uncles and cousins had been another stroke of luck, guaranteeing that Brynn would never be truly alone again, as she had been so often during her difficult childhood.

But Kelly loved Brynn too much to be anything but delighted for her recent blessings. And, besides, she reminded herself, she'd had a pretty good year as well. She had almost fully recovered from the devastating injuries of an auto accident that could have been totally debilitating, if not fatal. She was only months away from earning her master's degree. She had been instantly adopted into Brynn's family—both families, actually—and into Shane's group of friends. There was still plenty of time after she established her career to start her own family, something she wanted very badly. Assuming, of course, she was lucky enough to fall in love with someone as special as Brynn's Joe.

Brynn glanced at her watch, then chuckled. "We've been at the mall for nearly two hours and I still haven't bought the first Christmas present."

"Oops. My fault. I spent a long time trying to decide whether to buy the red dress."

Brynn shrugged. "I guess I'm just not really in the mood to Christmas shop today. I still have six weeks for that."

"We should at least buy one gift today," Kelly said firmly, picking up her coffee cup. "Then we can say we accomplished something."

Brynn smiled across the narrow table. "Just having a couple of hours together makes the day worthwhile. We're both so busy lately, it's rare for us to have time like this."

Kelly returned the smile. "Yes, and I've enjoyed every minute."

"Maybe we'll have time to shop a little more, though. Joe asked if I would mind buying both our draw gifts for my family. And I have no idea what to get for either of the people we drew."

Because the Walker family was so large and their income levels somewhat disparate, they had a long-standing tradition of drawing names for gift giving. The draw was held at the end of October, leaving everyone plenty of time to shop. Last year, newlywed Brynn had been included for the first time. And everyone had insisted that Kelly join in, to her surprise and delight. They had contended that she was an honorary member of the family, and she had come to feel that she truly belonged with them.

"Joe drew Taylor's name," Brynn confided. "I've got Shane. Do you have any clever ideas for either of them?"

Oddly enough, Kelly's pulse fluttered when Brynn mentioned Shane's name. Ignoring the reaction, she tried to reply casually. "I can see why you worry about finding the right gifts. Taylor has such impeccable taste, and Shane...well, he's Shane," she finished wryly.

Brynn laughed. "Strangely enough, I know exactly what you mean. Do me a favor, will you? You'll be seeing Shane several times between now and Christmas. You and he are such good friends. Try to get some suggestions from him about gift ideas—only, be subtle about it."

Kelly made a face. "Oh, sure. Piece of cake."

Still smiling, Brynn set her empty cappuccino cup aside. "I have every faith in you. Maybe I can get Taylor's partners at her advertising agency to give me some ideas for her. That would certainly make my shopping easier.''

''For everyone else to do the legwork for you? I guess it would make it easier for you,'' Kelly gibed teasingly.

''Hey, give me a break, okay? I haven't even started on the D'Alessandro family yet. They buy for *everyone*. I'm making Joe help with that undertaking.''

''And so you should.''

''At least I don't have to worry about what to get for his parents. Joe, Tony and Michael are chipping in to send their parents on a cruise after the first of the year.''

''Carla will love that,'' Kelly commented, picturing Joe's mother. A recently retired judge, Carla was still beautiful at seventy-one, and one of the most truly gracious women Kelly had ever met.

''So will Vinnie, though he probably won't admit it,'' Brynn said wryly, obviously very fond of her gruff but good-hearted retired-P.I. father-in-law.

Kelly reached for her purse and the package containing the new red dress she had *not* bought to impress anyone in particular. ''Okay,'' she said. ''Let's go shop.''

Brynn drew an exaggeratedly deep breath, as if for fortitude, and then stood. ''Look out, bargains, here we come. And Kelly, if you see anything Shane might like, be sure and point it out.''

Kelly reached up to ruffle her short, wispy blond hair, using the gesture as a ploy to avoid her friend's eyes. ''I don't know why you think I'd know what Shane likes, but I'll let you know if anything grabs me.''

''You want another soda?'' Shane asked Cameron as they lounged side by side on Shane's couch, their eyes focused on a televised football game.

Without looking away from the screen, Cameron replied. "No, I'm—damn, an interception!"

"Oh, man. He threw it right to the guy," Shane said in disgust.

They watched the resulting touchdown in glum resignation. All in all, they were having a great time, Shane thought with a wry smile.

The fishing trip hadn't lasted long. It had been quite cool that morning and the fish hadn't been in the mood to be caught. After a couple of hours, Shane and Cameron had returned to Shane's place, pulled out lunch meat, bread, chips, pickles and sodas, and had settled in front of the TV for an afternoon of food and football.

Lounging back against the couch cushions, Cameron laced his hands behind his head. "When is it you're supposed to baby-sit your kid sister?"

"Dad and Cassie are leaving the Saturday after Thanksgiving, and Molly's staying here with me for the next ten days."

Cameron shook his head. "I can't believe you volunteered for that. What do you know about taking care of little kids?"

"Molly's hardly an infant. She turned twelve a couple of weeks ago."

"Even worse." Cameron shuddered. "Hormones and stuff. I've heard of twelve-year-old girls getting pregnant."

"Not on my watch," Shane answered flatly. He'd pound any randy kid who came sniffing around his pretty seventh grade sister, he vowed. Actually, that sounded like a pretty good plan to follow for the next ten years or so.

"Okay, so maybe that was kind of extreme," Cameron admitted. "But you've got to admit you haven't had a lot of experience with kids."

"Molly and I lived in the same house from the time she was born until I left for college four years later. I've lived right next door to her since I built this house almost six years ago. I think I know her as well as anyone does. She's never given my folks a day of trouble."

"Yeah, well, who *would* give Jared any trouble? *I* still call him 'sir' and I don't even say that to my own father these days. I doubt that the kid is as intimidated by you as she is by your dad."

"Molly's hardly intimidated by Dad. She's got him wrapped around her little finger and she knows it."

"Yeah, but I bet she never gives him any back talk, either."

Shane had to concede that. As much as Jared doted on his little girl, he could be a stern parent when necessary. It had generally taken only a warning look to bring Shane in line, and the same held true with Molly.

Maybe Shane should be practicing some of those looks in the mirror.

Cameron glanced at the TV again. "Game's over. I lost twenty on it to a guy at work."

"Serves you right for taking a sucker bet."

"Thanks for the moral support, pal."

"You're welcome," Shane answered equably.

Cameron checked his watch. "I guess I should head home. You probably have some cowboy chores to do."

Chuckling at the wording, Shane shrugged. "I've got a few things to take care of. Why don't you hang around and help? I'll teach you how to milk a bull."

Cameron grunted. "Real funny, Walker."

"I suppose you have plans with Amber tonight."

"Er—no, actually. I told her I'd probably want to

crash after getting up so early for fishing. I need a night off.''

Shane didn't know quite what to say to that. He'd heard that note in Cameron's voice before—every time Cameron got tired of his latest girlfriend. When it came to women, Cameron had a very short attention span. He generally made an effort not to leave a string of broken hearts behind him, and had somehow managed to remain fairly good friends with most of his former lovers. But Shane wasn't sure that was going to be possible this time. Amber was so obviously besotted—and had been for a long time, even before Cameron had noticed. He had an unpleasant premonition that the affair between Cameron and Amber was not going to end as amicably as Cameron's previous liaisons.

"You're worried about Amber, aren't you?" Cameron asked, correctly interpreting his friend's silence.

He cleared his throat. "Well…maybe a little. She's been a good friend. I wouldn't want to see her hurt."

"Neither do I. I wish I could promise you it won't happen."

Shane studied his friend's face. "You're going to end it, aren't you?"

Squirming on the couch, Cameron looked away. "I haven't said that."

"Cam, think about who you're talking to. I was around for your first girlfriend, remember? I've been here for all of them since. I know when you're getting restless."

Cameron sighed. "It isn't working out. Amber's starting to hint about marriage and kids and, damn it, Shane, I'm just not ready for that. At first I thought maybe there was a chance…but I was fooling myself. And now it looks like I've gotten myself into a situation where I'm going to hurt her, no matter what I do.''

Shane winced. He'd known from the start that Amber wanted more than an affair with the man she'd been not-so-secretly in love with since she was a teenager. That had been back when Shane, Cameron, Scott and Heather had been in high school. Amber, a couple of years younger, had become a member of the group by being a friend of Heather's on the cheerleading squad. Her crush on Cameron—one of the ''coolest'' guys in high school—had been no secret to anyone except Cameron. Until recently.

It was going to be devastating for her to have come so close to her longtime dream, only to lose it again.

Shane couldn't even be angry with Cameron about it. He thought Cameron had really tried this time. He knew Cameron would rather cut off an arm than cause Amber pain. But the match had been ill-fated from the start, and unfortunately Cameron and Amber had been the only two involved who hadn't realized that until too late.

''I'm not going to break it off today,'' Cameron said in a feeble attempt at reassurance. ''I'll try a little longer to make it work. Maybe if I just give it a little more time…''

''Yeah,'' Shane said, aware that there was little confidence in his reply. ''Maybe so.''

Putting Cameron's problems out of his head, since there was nothing he could do about the situation, he changed the subject and Cameron gladly went along. Whatever happened, this friendship was solid, and neither of them could imagine anything that would bring it to an end.

On the Sunday before Thanksgiving, Kelly was invited to a D'Alessandro family gathering. Vinnie and

Carla D'Alessandro were delighted to have their entire family under one roof for lunch. Tony was there with his wife, Michelle, and their four children. Michael, an attorney who lived in Austin with his wife and daughter, had brought his family for the weekend, and would be staying through the holiday. And the youngest D'Alessandro brother, Joe, was spending his second holiday season with Brynn as his wife.

It was because of her close connection with Brynn that Kelly had been invited to the family gathering. The D'Alessandros were aware that Kelly had no family of her own with which to spend the holidays. For the same reason, the gregarious Walker clan was expecting her to join them for several holiday celebrations.

Because she had always been welcomed warmly and sincerely by both families, and had never been made to feel intrusive, she often accepted their invitations. It was so nice to feel as if she had family for the holidays, even if the connection was only an honorary one.

She returned to her apartment late that afternoon with a container of leftovers Carla had insisted she take home and a glow of contentment deep inside her. She'd had a lovely time with the D'Alessandro family, enjoying the noise and cheerful confusion. She'd been the first to slip away, claiming truthfully that she had several chores to attend to that evening. It was barely 6:00 p.m. when she pulled into her parking lot, but already quite dark. The night air chilled her as she climbed out of her car, reminding her that winter was just getting started.

She was still smiling to herself when she locked her faithful, no-frills little car. Her purse and the container of leftovers were tucked beneath her left arm. Her smile changed to a gasp of alarm when a hand fell on her shoulder. She came very close to dropping everything she held.

"I'm sorry. Did I startle you?"

Kelly put her right hand over her racing heart as she stared up at Shane. "No, you didn't startle me. You scared the spit out of me. What are you doing here?"

He smiled apologetically. "I brought your VCR. I figured out what was wrong with it and I think it will work fine now."

"Shane, you didn't have to come all the way in from the ranch just to return my VCR. I could have gotten it from you Thursday when we all come to the ranch for Thanksgiving."

He shrugged. "I had to come into town anyway. We had a water pump go out this morning and I had to find a part for it. I figured I might as well bring your VCR while I was at it."

She smiled weakly as her pulse rate slowly returned to normal. "Now that I've recovered from my heart attack, why don't we go inside?"

He squeezed her shoulder comfortingly, then released her. "I'll get your VCR out of my truck."

Shane carried the VCR into her apartment beneath one arm. He set it on its shelf next to her small TV. "It'll just take me a minute to hook this back up."

"I really appreciate this."

"No problem," he said, fiddling with cables.

"I'd like to repay you for the favor. Are you hungry? Will you stay for dinner?"

He gave her a lazy grin over his shoulder. "I'm always hungry. I would love to stay for dinner."

Something about that dimpled smile of his always made her insides quiver. During the past year, she'd become an expert at hiding that disconcerting reaction. She was able to respond with a suitably casual tone. "I'll get something started. Make yourself at home."

She didn't have to spend much time debating over what to make for dinner, both because there wasn't a lot to choose from in her sparsely furnished kitchen and because she knew what Shane liked. Pasta. The man would be perfectly content to eat pasta three meals a day—especially if he had something sweet to eat afterward.

She pulled a package of whole-wheat pasta out of the pantry. It wouldn't take her long to come up with a meal Shane would enjoy. She found herself humming softly as she started her cooking, aware of Shane moving around in the other room.

Half an hour later they sat at her table, plates of pasta with pesto sauce in front of them, a basket of crusty rolls between them. She'd found an apple pie in the freezer; it was in the oven now. The scent of apples and cinnamon wafted enticingly from the kitchen, and she noticed that Shane occasionally looked that way with a greedy gleam in his eyes.

As they ate, they talked about the day she had spent with the D'Alessandro family, all of whom Shane knew well. They talked about their friends and the ranch and Kelly's classes. They discussed the slate of offerings in the local movie theaters that weekend, a new country album they both liked, and the usual mess in Washington, D.C.

Chatting with Shane had always been easy for her. As a girl, she had often fantasized about having an older brother. During the past year and a half, she had tried to think of Shane that way—or maybe as a favorite cousin—but she couldn't quite pull that off. She thought of him, instead, as a very special friend.

They ate dessert in front of the TV. On the pretext of making sure the VCR was working correctly, Shane had brought a video along. It was one he knew she hadn't seen, an action-packed "buddy film" not usually to her taste. Shane had assured her several times that she would like this one, and she did...until the end, when one of the two dashing heroes died heroically and, for Kelly, unexpectedly. She sniffled through the remaining minutes of the video, which ended happily for the other hero and his love interest.

When the credits began to roll, Shane pushed the stop button and started the rewind process. And then he looked at Kelly and chuckled. "You're crying."

She dashed at her face with the heel of her hand. "I am not."

Smiling indulgently, he slung an arm around her shoulders and used his other hand to wipe a tear from her cheek. "It was only a movie, Kelly. Nobody really died," he teased.

"I'm aware of that," she replied with as much dignity as she could summon considering that she was practically in his arms, her eyes still moist from her emotional response to the video. "It just got to me a little, that's all."

He used his fingertips to brush away the last remaining traces of her tears. "Anyone ever tell you that you're a marshmallow, Kelly Morrison?"

Since she'd always been embarrassingly sentimental, tearing up over sad movies, sweet love songs, mushy greeting cards and even sappy television commercials, Kely had to confess ruefully, "Yeah. More than a few times."

"It's one of the things I like best about you," he assured her, and leaned over to kiss her cheek. Somehow the kiss went astray, landing at the corner of her mouth instead.

She felt her eyes widen, felt her breath lodge somewhere deep in her chest. Shane drew away only a fraction of an inch, his gaze locked with hers, a startled expression in his eyes. And then his mouth was on hers, and he was kissing her in a way he had never kissed her before.

There was nothing familial about this kiss. Nothing brotherly or even cousinly. It was the kind of kiss a man gives a woman he finds attractive.

Kelly's first reaction was sheer pleasure. This, she thought dazedly, her hands settling tentatively on Shane's shoulders, was one amazing kiss.

Her second reaction was pure panic. What on earth was Shane *doing?*

Chapter Four

The impulsive kiss didn't last very long. Kelly ended it almost as soon as it began, breaking away with a jerk and a loud gasp.

Shane might have predicted surprise from her. Even displeasure, perhaps. What he had *not* expected to see in her eyes was fear.

Typically his first impulse in response to an uncertain situation was to make a joke. "Well, that was—"

Kelly jumped to her feet as if the sofa cushions had suddenly burst into flames. "It's late," she said, her voice a half octave higher than usual. "You'd better go."

Rising more slowly, he reached out a hand, intending to give her shoulder a reassuring squeeze. "Kelly..."

She flinched away as if he had threatened to strike her. Before he could ask what on earth was wrong with her, she snatched his jacket from the coat rack and practically threw it at him. "Thanks again for fixing my VCR. Tell your parents and Molly I said hello."

There was an odd edge to her babbling. In anyone else, Shane might have called it hysteria. "What the hell is wrong with you?"

Avoiding his eyes, she reached for the doorknob. "I'm tired. And I have an early class tomorrow. I need to…"

"Kelly." He covered her hand with his before she could open the door. "It was only a kiss."

He felt a tremor go through her. "I know. It shouldn't have happened."

He frowned. He hadn't planned to kiss her, it had just happened somehow. But she didn't have to act like it was such a terrible thing. "It was only a kiss," he repeated a bit lamely.

She shook his hand off hers and opened the door. "Don't do it again," she muttered, still without looking at him.

A minute later, he found himself outside her apartment, blinking at the door she had just closed between them. "That," he said to the darkness around him, "was just weird."

He thought about that kiss, and Kelly's overreaction to it, during the entire drive home. Sure, the kiss had been unexpected. An impulse he couldn't explain even if he were to try. They'd been having such a warm, pleasant evening and she had looked so sweet and pretty with her sentimental tears on her cheek, and she'd felt so good in his arms and…well, things had sort of gotten out of hand. But it hadn't seemed so bad to him—in fact, it had been a great kiss while it had lasted.

Funny. Had he thought about kissing Kelly before, he might have imagined it would be something like kissing one of his cousins. Or one of the women in his circle of pals. He hadn't thought it would make his blood pump faster or his head start spinning.

No matter how great a kiss it had been—or might have been had it lasted a bit longer—it wasn't something he intended to repeat. For one thing, it was simply too awkward, considering their family connections. And Kelly had made it clear enough that she had no intention for it to happen again. She had made that *very* clear, he thought, frowning as he remembered the way she had practically kicked him out of her apartment.

He could take a hint. No more stolen kisses between him and Kelly. Definitely a sensible plan.

But damn, that had been a good kiss.

Kelly was so tired Monday afternoon that all she planned to do that evening was crash in front of the television and try to lose herself in totally mindless entertainment. She didn't want to see anyone or talk to anyone or even think about anyone in particular. She just wanted to escape the tension that had gripped her ever since Shane kissed her.

She knew exactly what that tension was rooted in. Fear. She was terrified that something would change. Something that would threaten the happy contentment she'd found since moving to Dallas and making a home for herself here.

After a dinner of canned soup and a green salad, she had just settled onto her couch with a paperback romance and the TV remote when her doorbell chimed, disturbing her solitude. She groaned, and her chest clenched. She was afraid she would find Shane on the other side of her door. For the first time since she met him, she wasn't at all sure she wanted to see him.

But when she looked through the peephole, it wasn't Shane she found on her doorstep. The relief she felt was tempered by a faint disappointment that made no sense to her at all.

"Amber," she said, opening the door. "What are you—what's wrong?"

Tears streaming down her face, Amber hiccuped on a sob. "Cameron...Cameron..."

Her voice broke.

Kelly knew immediately what had happened. She had been expecting this, she thought sadly. Her heart twisting in response to Amber's obvious pain, she reached out to take her friend's hands. "Come in," she said, tugging gently. "Sit down. I'll make us some tea. Then we'll talk."

Shane was in the barn with Molly, both of them bent over a horse's swollen fetlock. "It's looking a lot better," Shane assured his worried little sister. "He should be completely recovered in a couple of days."

Her pretty young face creased with a frown beneath a wispy fringe of red bangs, Molly looked anxiously up at him. "You're sure? He's really going to be okay?"

"I'm sure." He reached out to give her a bracing, one-armed hug. "He's already a lot better than he was yesterday."

Reassured, Molly beamed up at him. And, as always, Shane was warmed by the sight of her bright, beautiful smile. "I'm glad he's going to be okay," she said.

"So am I, Little Bit." He brushed his lips across the upturned tip of her gold-dusted nose. "Now you'd better go in and get busy with your homework. I'll finish up out—"

"Hey, Shane."

Both Shane and Molly turned quickly toward the door. Shane lifted his eyebrows in surprise when he saw Cameron North standing in the doorway of the barn. "Hey, Cam. What's up?"

Cameron's smile was only a faint shadow of his usual grin. "How's it going, beautiful?" he asked Molly, evading Shane's question.

"Hi, Cameron." As susceptible to Cameron's charms as most other females, Molly broke away from her brother and almost skipped across the barn to greet his friend. "I didn't know you were coming today."

"Neither did Shane. It's a surprise visit."

Shane noticed with fraternal disapproval that there was a hint of experimental flirtation in Molly's expressive green eyes when she smiled up at Cameron. "It's a very nice surprise," she said. "I haven't seen you in a long time."

He tugged affectionately at one of her braids. "Blame that on your busy social life. Seems like every time I come to visit, you're off on a big date."

Molly giggled. "Not a date. Daddy said I can't date until I'm fifteen."

"Dad said you can't date until you're thirty," Shane corrected her. "Your mom said fifteen. Maybe."

Molly rolled her eyes. "That's still three whole years away."

"Don't be in such a hurry to get started on that path," Cameron advised her, his smile looking forced. "Trust me, it's a lot more fun being friends than trying to turn it into something more."

Shane grimaced. He knew now why Cameron had shown up, looking so uncharacteristically morose.

"Molly, you'd better head inside to get busy with that homework," he said, patting his sister's shoulder. "I

promised Cassie I'd send you in before dark. Tell Dad
I'll talk to him later, okay?''

"Okay. Bye, Cameron.''

"See you later, gorgeous.''

Blushing and giggling, Molly hurried away. Looking
after her, Cameron shook his head. "She's growing up
too fast, Shane.''

Since it seemed like only yesterday that his little sister
had been a diapered toddler, Shane nodded gravely.
"Dad and I have done everything but put a brick on her
head to keep her from growing any faster, but I guess
we're losing the battle.''

Cameron pushed his hands into the pockets of his
fashionably loose khaki slacks. "You got much more to
do tonight?''

Shane latched the stall door behind him as he moved
toward Cameron, leaving the injured horse to loudly
munch grain. "No. I was just finishing up out here.''

"Do you have any plans for the evening?''

"I was thinking about grilling a steak and crashing in
front of *Monday Night Football*. Want to join me?''

Cameron nodded acceptance to the casual invitation.
"I'd like that.''

"Okay—but you have to cook your own steak.''

"I can handle that. Maybe,'' Cameron added with a
wry smile.

They fell into step as they left the barn side by side.

"I just want to die.'' It was about the tenth time Amber had said that in the hour and a half since she'd shown
up on Kelly's doorstep.

Kelly handed her friend another tissue. "No, you
don't,'' she said for at least the tenth time in return.
"You're in pain, but you don't really want to die.''

Amber drew a shuddering breath and made a visible effort to pull herself together. "I guess you're right," she conceded in a mumble. "But I don't know how I'm going to get past this."

"You'll get past it by holding your head up and going on with your life," Kelly told her firmly. "I have no doubt that you can do it."

Amber gave a sigh that seemed to come from the bottom of her soul. "It's just that I had so hoped Cameron would always be a part of my future."

"I know. And I'm sorry it isn't going to happen the way you wanted it to."

Twisting her fingers in her lap, Amber sniffed. "I've dreamed of marrying Cameron ever since I was sixteen. For a little while, I thought my dream was going to come true."

Kelly hesitated, then asked carefully, "Did you really think that? Did you really believe you and Cameron would be married and settle down for the rest of your lives together?"

Amber opened her mouth to answer, and then she, too, paused, biting her lip. "Maybe not," she admitted after a moment. "Even when Cameron and I were together, I knew deep inside that it couldn't last. He's just…he's not…"

Kelly understood what her friend was trying to say. Cameron wasn't exactly the home-and-hearth type. Kelly couldn't really imagine him getting married and mowing a lawn or attending a PTA meeting. The footloose reporter was a confirmed bachelor, and Kelly had never really believed his feelings for Amber—whatever they had been—were strong enough to change him.

"You knew it wasn't going to work out, didn't you?" Amber asked, studying Kelly's face.

She chose her words with care. "I wanted it to work. For your sake."

"But you didn't think it would."

"I just didn't know."

Amber wrapped her arms around herself and rocked miserably on the couch. "The holidays are going to be so awful. I told everyone Cameron would be there for our family Thanksgiving dinner. You know he isn't close to his own parents, so I just assumed..."

Kelly wondered if it was dread of the upcoming holidays that had prompted Cameron to end the relationship that afternoon. He probably thought it would be entirely too awkward to go through the season as a couple when he knew all along that it couldn't lead where Amber wanted it to go.

Amber shuddered. "It's going to be so uncomfortable seeing him again when we all get together. How am I supposed to play games with him and socialize with him as if nothing happened between us? What will I do if I go to a party and Cameron's there with a...with a date?"

"I don't know."

"I hate him for doing this to me." Amber's mood shifted mercurially from grief to fury. "How could he lead me on the way he did when he *knew* how I felt about him? He let me hope—and then he just ended it. 'We can still be friends,' he said. I don't *want* to be his friend. I'm friends with Shane and Scott and Michael. Cameron is different."

To be fair, Kelly thought Cameron hadn't really known how Amber felt about him. Amber had simply decided several months ago to go after him, to take a chance at pursuing her longtime infatuation. She'd somehow convinced him to give them a chance, and maybe for a while he'd really wanted it to work out, but

Kelly suspected that Cameron had broken it off as soon as he was certain it wasn't going to last. "I hope you and Cameron will find a way to be friends again. You've known each other so long."

"I've wasted most of that time being in love with him. And he just let me go on loving him, until he finally decided to temporarily take what I was offering. Then when he got tired of me, he just expected to pat me on the head and have everything go back to the way it was. Now I'm just supposed to smile and say nothing while he goes back to chasing one bimbo after another."

That tirade, of course, was quite unfair, since Amber had been the one to initiate the affair—but Kelly bit back her automatic impulse to defend Cameron. "What else can you do?" she asked logically.

Amber promptly burst into tears again.

This, Kelly thought, patting her friend's heaving shoulder, was exactly why she had panicked when Shane kissed her. There was nothing sadder than a couple who ruined a wonderful friendship with romance. She'd seen it happen too many times, and it was almost impossible for everything to go back to the way it had been before. In her experience, it almost always ended in disaster. Just look at how unhappy Amber was now, she thought. And imagine how awkward it would be when they all got together again—*if* they all ever got together again.

Nothing, she thought glumly, could ruin a wonderful relationship faster than an ill-advised romance. She had no intention of getting involved in anything that foolish herself.

"So then I told her there's no way I'm spending all day Thanksgiving being stared at and cross-examined by her parents, siblings, grandparents, aunts, uncles, cousins and neighbors. There really wasn't any point to it, I said, because I couldn't see me ever spending more time with her family anyway. That's when she gave me this sort of wounded look and said something about when we were married…and I guess I lost it. I told her marriage wasn't an option for us—for me, really—and I was sorry if she had gotten another idea. Then she started crying and calling me names, and before I knew it, doors were slamming and the whole thing was over.''

Sitting in a chair watching Cameron pace the living room, Shane listened to the tale without an outward re-action, though he cringed on the inside as he pictured how unpleasant the scene must have been. ''Sorry, Cam, I know it must have been hard for you.''

''That's an understatement,'' Cameron growled. ''It was sheer hell. I tried, Shane, I really did. But when she started talking about marriage…''

Shane nodded. This has been inevitable, he thought. He couldn't imagine Cameron marrying *anyone,* cer-tainly not Amber. But he hated that it had to go down this way, for both their sakes.

''Is there anything I can do?''

Cameron turned to look at him. ''You're doing it,'' he answered quietly. ''Thanks for listening.''

Somewhat awkwardly Shane shrugged. ''You would do the same for me.''

Cameron snorted and ran a hand through his heavy gold hair. ''Like you'd ever end up in a mess like this. You've never made a stupid mistake with a woman. Probably never will.''

Shane swallowed, thinking uncomfortably of a certain unplanned kiss. ''I've made my share of blunders.''

''Maybe. But not like the ones I've gotten myself into,'' Cameron countered glumly. ''You've always been too careful and too firmly rooted here with your family and your ranch to waste time in self-destructive relationships.''

Shane wondered what Cameron would think if he confided that his caution was due more to fear than discretion. Shane had always worried about getting involved in a relationship as disastrous as his parents' marriage, or his mother's second marriage. He had seen firsthand how miserable people could make each other. How others could suffer from mistakes made in the name of love.

He had long since decided that he would never even consider marriage unless he found what his father had found with Cassie. A love so strong, so intense, that it was almost palpable. A commitment so deep and so binding that nothing beyond death could break it.

Rather embarrassed by the direction his thoughts had taken, and relieved that Cameron couldn't read his mind, Shane cleared his throat. ''So what are you going to do now?''

Lifting one shoulder, Cameron replied. ''I suppose I'll try to avoid her for a while—until she cools off some. Maybe, after that, we can figure out a way to be friends again. But that's all. Just friends.''

Cameron had been successful in the past turning lovers into friends. But this time, Shane wondered if it was possible for Cameron and Amber to go back to a comfortably platonic relationship. The affair had been too hot, too fast, too intense. Too big a mistake from the beginning.

As Shane sat back and listened quietly while Cameron continued to unload his frustrations, he fervently hoped *he* would never be so unfortunate as to get involved in something that ill-advised and painful.

* * *

Thanksgiving Day dawned crisp, clear and beautiful. No one could have asked for more perfect holiday weather. Kelly should have been delighted to be on her way to a big family holiday meal, the kind she had always fantasized about as a child. The Walker siblings always had such a good time when they got together. She had enjoyed their get-togethers since the first one she had attended, when she was still in a wheelchair after her accident. She had looked forward to each gathering since, especially when they were held at the Walker ranch, as this one would be.

But that had been before Shane kissed her.

She was determined not to let that single incident change anything. As Shane had pointed out, it had only been a kiss, and a brief one at that. There was no reason for them to mention it again—no purpose in even thinking about it. She, for one, intended to act as if nothing had happened.

"Is anything bothering you, Kelly?" Brynn asked, twisting in the front seat of her husband's car to look at Kelly, who sat in the back seat.

Kelly pasted on a smile. "Not at all. Why do you ask?"

"You seem preoccupied today. You have ever since we picked you up."

Kelly shook her head. "I'm fine. But thanks for asking."

Tucking a strand of chestnut-brown hair behind her ear, Brynn studied Kelly's face for another moment, as if she wasn't quite satisfied with her friend's denial. Joe spoke before his wife could question their passenger further. "How's school going, Kelly?"

"Finals are coming up. And then I'm one semester away from my degree," she announced with satisfaction.

Her education had been hard-won, obtained with un-wavering determination and single-minded purpose. She loved the job she would be doing when she finished, working with hearing- and speech-impaired children, and she had already made several valuable contacts to-ward finding a permanent position.

Brynn made a face. "I'll be glad when I can say I only have one semester left toward my degree. I still have two semesters to go after this one—and then at least a year of postgraduate work."

It had been somewhat easier for Kelly to attend col-lege than it had been for Brynn. Kelly had had some life insurance money left in a trust fund by her mother, who died when Kelly was thirteen. She'd also received small monthly child support checks from her career-military father, whom she hadn't seen since she was a child. Those checks had stopped several years ago, but they, along with the trust fund and academic scholarships, had funded Kelly's college education.

Brynn, whose teenage father had died before her birth and whose emotionally troubled young mother had left no insurance money behind when she'd taken her own life, had been dependent upon child welfare services to provide for her until she'd turned eighteen. Since then, she'd been on her own, working her way slowly toward a degree in education by taking an occasional evening class and working in day-care centers during the days. When Kelly had been accepted into UT-Dallas, she'd talked Brynn into moving with her, assuring her the job opportunities would be better here for both of them than in Longview, where they'd lived previously.

Instead, they'd been hit head-on by a speeding drunken driver before they'd even unpacked their bags, and Dr. Joe D'Alessandro, a witness to the crash, had come into their lives. He had operated on Kelly's mangled legs and had fallen in love with Brynn. And now Brynn was able to attend classes full-time, her goal of being an elementary school teacher finally within sight.

"How's Amber?" Brynn asked, changing the subject. "Have you talked to her since Monday?"

"She called last night. She's still an emotional wreck, but I made her promise to try to enjoy Thanksgiving with her family today."

"And Cameron? Have you heard from him?"

Kelly shook her head. "No. I'm sure Shane has talked to him, but I haven't spoken with Shane this week, so I don't know how Cameron's doing."

"Probably just fine," Brynn said in disapproval. "I doubt that he's eating his heart out like poor Amber. This sort of thing is almost routine for Cameron."

"Cameron isn't heartless," Kelly protested. "I'm sure he hated hurting Amber. But he would have hurt her worse if he had let it go on longer when it just wasn't working for him."

Brynn peered over the seat back. "You're defending him rather heatedly. Are you sure *you* don't have a thing for Cameron?"

"Brynn," Joe murmured.

Brynn shrugged unrepentantly. "You should have heard the way she grilled me about *you* before you and I got together. She knew I was besotted with you, and she teased me mercilessly about it."

"You were besotted, huh?" Joe seemed to like that description.

"Oh, very," Brynn answered humorously. "Of course, that was before I married you."

"Are you saying you aren't still besotted?"

With wide eyes and a broad smile, Brynn patted his

arm. "I am still most definitely besotted," she assured. Then, without pausing, she asked, "What about you, Kelly? Are you besotted with Cameron North?"

"No," she said firmly. "I am not besotted, infatuated or in any other way taken with Cameron. He's a friend, that's all. And I don't think he should have to take all the blame for a relationship that was always destined to fail."

She, Kelly assured herself, was not besotted with *anyone*. And she would just as soon keep it that way for now.

The talk turned to other topics, and inevitably Joe turned onto the road that led to the Walker ranch. The closer they came, the more tension Kelly felt building inside her. She had practically thrown Shane out of her apartment Sunday evening. She hadn't heard from him since. Would the awkward incident cause him to treat her differently today than usual? Would the others notice, and wonder why?

She had her answer as soon as she climbed out of the car. "Hey, Kelly! Heads up," she heard Shane yell.

She turned, and was nearly hit in the face with a football. She caught it at the last moment, using reflexes she hadn't known she had.

"Shane!" His aunt, Michelle, who had seen the incident as she'd hurried to greet Brynn, Joe and Kelly, scolded him as if he were seventeen rather than ten years older. "You nearly hit Kelly in the face with that ball. She could have been hurt."

"Not Kelly," Shane answered with an impudent grin. "She moves pretty fast when she wants to."

"Besides which," Kelly replied, deciding to follow his lead with joking, "if you *had* hit me in the face, I would have made you eat this football."

Michelle's eleven-year-old son, Jason, laughed. "She sounds pretty scary, Shane. You'd better watch out."

"She is scary," Shane answered with a laugh, taking the football back from Kelly and then ruffling her hair. "But I like her, anyway."

"Me, too," Jason's little sister, Katie, who'd been tagging behind the others, declared. She threw her arms around Kelly's legs and beamed up at her. "Kelly's nice."

"Thank you, Katie." Kelly was touched by the six-year-old's ingenuous gesture. "I like you, too."

"Do you like Shane?"

Kelly briefly met Shane's eyes, finding nothing there but amusement. If he even remembered the incident Sunday night, he wasn't letting it show. "Yes, I like Shane, too," she replied casually. Then added in a stage whisper to the little girl, "*Most* of the time."

Katie giggled. Shane and Jason laughed aloud. And Kelly, relieved that everything seemed to be just the same as always, turned to help Brynn and Joe unload the food they had brought with them for the Thanksgiving celebration.

Chapter Five

During the first twenty minutes after they arrived, Kelly, Brynn and Joe were greeted by a dizzying number of family members. Though the six surviving Walker siblings had been orphaned and separated as small children, they had become very close during the years that had passed since they'd found each other again. All six had married and had produced a total of fourteen offspring—not counting Brynn, the daughter of the one brother who hadn't survived for the reunion. All but one sister, Lindsay Grant, lived near Dallas, Texas. Lindsay and her family lived in neighboring Arkansas, but visited as often as their busy schedules allowed.

Everyone had been able to attend this Thanksgiving Day gathering, which meant there was total chaos at the Walker ranch—adults talking, laughing and good-naturedly arguing, children running, squealing and occasionally crying, dogs barking and horses whinnying. No one there would have had it any other way.

The traditional Thanksgiving fare of turkey and all the trimmings—side dishes provided potluck-style by the guests—was served on the tree-shaded back lawn, where several long tables and plenty of folding chairs had been set up. The weather had cooperated nicely; it was sunny and warm enough that a sweater or light jacket was all anyone needed. An occasional breeze toyed with the crisp white tablecloths and carried the tantalizing aromas of the food and the more delicate scent of the masses of fall flowers Cassie had used for centerpieces.

It had always seemed natural for the young singles in the family to cluster together. Shane, the eldest at twenty-seven, usually held court at the "singles table." He did the same on this day, insisting that Kelly take the chair at his right. His cousins, the Samples siblings, joined them—twenty-one-year-old Dawne and eighteen-year-old Keith, both college students, and Brittany, a fifteen-year-old high school sophomore. There was a newcomer at the table this year, sixteen-year-old Emilio Ramirez, a foster son of Shane's Aunt Lindsay and her husband, Dr. Nick Grant.

Painfully shy and recently orphaned, Emilio seemed a bit dazed by the pandemonium of the Walker Thanksgiving celebration. It took Shane less than twenty minutes to have the young man joining shyly in the conversation, looking almost happy to be there.

"He's something else, isn't he?" Dawne murmured into Kelly's ear.

Kelly turned to the young woman beside her. "Who?"

"Shane." Dawne nodded toward her cousin, who was practicing his rather rusty Spanish, to Emilio's obvious amusement. "He's already got that boy feeling like a member of the family."

"Shane's very good at putting people at ease," Kelly agreed quietly. "I remember the first time he visited me in the hospital. He was a complete stranger to me, but he'd heard about the accident and he thought I might be lonely and afraid, so he and Jared stopped by to visit when they made a trip into Dallas for supplies. By the time they left, I felt like I'd known them for ages."

"I have to admit, I adore Shane," Dawne said with a sigh. "It's just too darned bad he's my cousin. Sometimes I wonder if I'll ever meet a guy as special as he is."

"Of course you'll meet someone," Kelly assured the wholesomely attractive college senior.

"When I do, I hope he's just like Shane. Sweet and funny and kind and good-natured. He loves kids and animals and little old ladies. Have you ever even seen him lose his temper?"

Kelly had to think about that for a minute. "Well, no, actually, I haven't," she finally admitted. There had been times when she'd thought Shane was a bit annoyed with someone, but she'd never seen him really angry.

"Neither have I," Dawne responded. "And I've known him since he was fourteen."

Kelly looked assessingly at Shane, wondering if he truly was that easygoing or if his temper, like his emotions, remained hidden behind his lazy, unrevealing smiles.

He glanced her way, their gazes meeting. "What are you two talking about so seriously?"

"You," Kelly answered equably.

"Good. I like it when you talk about me."

"You just like being the center of everyone's attention," Dawne accused him affectionately.

"Exactly."

An outburst from the kids' table, around which ten children under the age of twelve were gathered, claimed everyone's attention then. While parents rushed to deal with the situation, everyone else continued their meals and their spirited conversations.

Watching as Shane turned back to chat with Emilio, it occurred to Kelly that Dawne was right. Shane *was* a very special guy. And if *she* ever met anyone, she, too, wouldn't mind if he was a lot like Shane.

The "outsider attack" came completely without warning, catching Kelly totally unprepared. One minute she was contently mingling with the thirty or so members of the extended Walker clan, and the next minute she was on the outside of the family circle, gazing wistfully in.

It was only in her own mind, of course. Everyone treated her as warmly and graciously as they ever did. But suddenly she found herself fighting those old childhood demons—fear of rejection, of humiliation, of not fitting in.

Annoyed with herself for giving in to such groundless neuroses, she drifted toward the barn, thinking maybe a visit with the horses would give her time to bolster her self-confidence. She apparently wasn't the only one who'd had the idea. "Emilio," she said to the slender young man gazing into one of the stalls. "Do you like horses?"

The boy jumped and whirled to face her. "I didn't touch anything. I was only looking at the horses."

She smiled reassuringly. "It's okay. Jared and Shane

don't mind you looking. In fact, they would probably take you for a ride if you want."

"I've never ridden a horse before."

"No?" Moving slowly to allow him to recover from the start she'd given him, she leaned against the stall railing beside him. "What *have* you ridden?"

"Dirt bikes. I used to race them. My dad…" The boy choked.

"Your father helped you race?" Kelly supplied gently, her heart twisting in compassion.

Emilio nodded. "He died two years ago. My mother died when I was a baby. I lived with my grandmother for a year, but she was old and sick."

"I'm sorry, Emilio. You've had a very difficult time, haven't you?"

He shrugged and looked at the dozing horse again.

"Do you like living with Lindsay and Nick?"

"They're nice," he conceded hesitantly. "Dr. Nick used to race bikes, and he said he'll help me get started again in the spring—if I'm still with them then. They treat me good. Better than the last place."

"They're nice people. And their children are so sweet."

"They're okay," the teenager conceded about the eight-year-old daughter and six-year-old son of his foster parents. "They sure have a lot of family," he added. "At least, Lindsay does."

Kelly chuckled softly. "Yes, Lindsay has two complete families. This one—her biological siblings—and the parents and two brothers who adopted her as a baby. Not to mention all the foster sons her adoptive parents took in over the years. She considers them all family, and she loves them all."

"She has a big heart."

"Yes," Kelly agreed with a smile, thinking that Emilio had fallen quickly for his foster mother. "She does."

Emilio looked at the horse again. "Everyone has been very nice to me here. But you have so many cousins. It makes me…"

"Dizzy?" Kelly supplied for him with a smile. "I know the feeling. This isn't my family, Emilio. They aren't my cousins. I'm a foster kid, too."

He looked at her in surprise. "*You* are?"

"I used to be. When my mother became too ill to take care of me, I was placed into a foster home with Brynn D'Alessandro, Lindsay's niece. Brynn and I have remained close friends and I've gotten to know her family very well during the past couple of years. They're wonderful. But I still know how you feel. Sometimes I'm very much aware that I have no family connection to the others."

His dark chocolate eyes focused intently on her face. "I would never have known you aren't related to them."

"Most of the adult members of this family have been in foster care at one time or another. And Jared and Cassie, who own this ranch along with Shane, have taken in foster sons several times during the past few years, though they don't have one in residence at the moment. They know how important it is to make newcomers feel welcome. And they know it is always possible to make room in the family for more."

Emilio thought about her words for a moment, and then smiled. "It's a nice family."

"Yes," Kelly agreed, and she was glad now that she had chosen to come to the barn. Both she and Emilio had needed this talk.

The boy's smile suddenly turned a bit mischievous, making him look more his age than the somber expression he'd worn before had. "But can you name them all?"

"Not only can I name them, I can do it in order." Lifting her chin in response to the challenge, Kelly drew a deep breath. "Jared's the eldest. He's married to Cassie, and they have Shane and Molly. Then there's Layla, who married Kevin Samples and had Dawne, Keith and Brittany. A brother named Miles died on his eighteenth birthday. His daughter—my friend, Brynn—was born after he died. She married Joe D'Alessandro. Then come the twins—Joe Walker, who's married to Lauren and has a little boy named Casey, and Ryan Walker, who married Taylor and has twin boys, Andrew and Aaron. Michelle and her husband, Tony D'Alessandro, have four children, Jason, Carly, Katie and Justin. And finally there's your foster family, Lindsay, who married Nick Grant, and their two children, Jenny and Clay." She finished on her last gasp of breath.

Emilio laughed. "Okay, I'm impressed."

"And so am I." Shane stepped out of the shadows of the barn, his eyes on Kelly.

Emilio stiffened. "We were just looking at the horses," he said quickly.

Kelly wondered what in Emilio's background made him go so quickly on the defensive. Had he often been falsely accused of misdeeds?

"How would you like to take a ride?" Shane offered.

The boy's face lit with a mixture of excitement and trepidation. "I don't know how."

Shane clapped him on the shoulder. "You'll know by the time you leave here today," he promised.

Shane had begun to wonder if he would ever have a chance to talk to Kelly in private that day. It seemed that there was never a moment when they weren't surrounded by other people. Either it was simply coincidence—not so hard to believe, considering the number of guests that day—or Kelly was taking pains to keep from being alone with him.

He wasn't at all pleased by that possibility.

From several yards away, he watched as she organized a game of Simon Says with the children late that afternoon. She looked particularly nice today, he thought, admiring the pumpkin-colored sweater that clung so enticingly to her small, firm breasts, and the way her dark indigo jeans cupped her tight bottom. He wouldn't have been a normal male if he hadn't noticed those details, along with the attractive flush of pink in her smooth, fair cheeks and the glittering strawberry highlights in her short, tousled blond hair. He'd always liked long hair on other women, but Kelly's wispy cut suited her, emphasizing her big green eyes and slender throat.

He suddenly frowned and shifted his weight, shoving his hands into the front pockets of his jeans. Damn, what was this? Surely he wasn't standing here getting all warm and itchy just from looking at Kelly. And why was he suddenly remembering the way she'd felt in his arms, the taste of her mouth beneath his?

What the hell was going on between them lately? Why was he suddenly having trouble thinking of Kelly as just another member of the family? Or was this really all that sudden? The truth was, he'd been drawn to her since the day he'd first seen her lying in a hospital bed, broken and hurting, but with a spark of spirit in her emerald eyes that had refused to be extinguished.

Okay. So they were exceptionally good friends, he told himself. Such close bonds were rare and precious.

He wasn't about to screw things up, the way Cameron had with Amber.

But he still wanted a chance to talk to Kelly alone.

He found that opportunity soon after her game with the children ended. It was getting cooler as the day wore on, and the guests were beginning to drift inside the ranch house. No one seemed in a hurry to leave, and soon they would pull out the leftovers from lunch for an evening meal. Always the conscientious hostess, Cassie suggested organizing various games, grouped by age and interest, in several rooms of her house. Charades in the living room, poker in the den, board games on the dining room table, Trivial Pursuit in the extra room they used as a computer room and library. Football games were tuned in on a couple of different television sets for those who chose to watch rather than play.

"Shane, we're almost out of canned soft drinks," Cassie commented, pushing her unruly mop of red hair away from her face, which was still fresh and unlined as she approached her fortieth birthday.

Giving his stepmother an affectionate smile, he nodded. "I'll go fetch the ones we stashed in my fridge. Kelly, can you give me a hand?" he asked, as if on a sudden impulse.

He saw what might have been a quick flare of nerves in her eyes, but she masked it quickly and nodded. "Sure. I'd be glad to."

Cassie smiled in satisfaction. "Thanks, you two. I appreciate it. Now I'd better go make sure everyone's found something interesting to do."

"Cassie's such a good hostess," Kelly commented as she and Shane began the quarter-mile walk to his house. "She's so careful to make sure everyone has a good time."

"She enjoys entertaining. Dad's gotten accustomed to having a crowd underfoot—even seems to like it most of the time." Shane knew how much adjustment it had taken for his father, who'd been a loner all his life, to suddenly find himself part of a large, demonstrative family. Shane had taken to their new life immediately, but Jared had needed a bit more encouragement. He'd found that motivation in his love for Cassie.

Paulie, the border collie, came running up to meet them as they approached Shane's house. Shane absently patted the dog's black-and-white head. Kelly greeted him with more affection, bending down to stroke him into a frenzy of delight. "Good dog," she said. "You're such a sweet boy."

Shane had a sudden image of those soft hands stroking *his* body. He cleared his throat abruptly. "Do you like kittens?"

With a final pat for the dog, Kelly straightened. "Who doesn't like kittens?"

"Lots of people. There's a new litter on my back porch if you want to see them. A pregnant stray showed up a couple of weeks ago and Molly talked me into letting her stay."

"Marshmallow."

He sighed. "Yeah, I know."

"How many kittens did she have?"

"Three."

"And Paulie doesn't bother them?"

"Paulie's used to all kinds of different critters being around. Molly would have a whole zoo if Dad and Cassie would let her."

Kelly took one look at the furry family nesting on Shane's back porch and fell instantly in love. Shane stood to one side and observed indulgently as she fell to her knees beside the bed he'd fashioned from a cardboard box lined with old towels. The mother cat, surprisingly friendly for a stray, made no effort to stop Kelly from admiring the babies.

Shane found himself getting aroused all over again as he watched Kelly run a fingertip slowly over a soft, sleeping little body, a look of sheer delight on her face, her eyes soft with pleasure. He shifted his weight, drawing her attention away from the kittens for a moment.

"They're precious," she crooned. "Especially the little white one with the gray spots. Are they boys or girls?"

"The white one is female, I think, and the two gray-striped ones male. It's hard to tell with kittens, but that's my best guess."

She looked down at the kittens again. "They're so sweet. I always wanted a cat when I was growing up."

"Why didn't you have one?"

"My mother was too ill to deal with pets when I was little. And then I moved in with Mrs. Fendel, who was allergic to cats."

"There's nothing to stop you from having a cat now, is there?"

She looked intrigued. "I don't know. I haven't given it much thought."

Kneeling beside her, he gently lifted the white-and-gray kitten. He placed it in Kelly's hands. "This little girl needs a home."

Temptation warred for a moment with wariness, and then Kelly smiled and lifted the mewing little creature to her cheek. "Will you teach me how to take care of her?"

"You bet. It isn't that hard. Cats are pretty self-sufficient. She'll need her shots in a few weeks and you'll want to have her spayed as soon as she's old enough—just as I'll have the males neutered before I find homes for them. After that, it's just a matter of giving her affection and attention and yearly booster shots.''

''When will she be old enough to leave her mother?''

''A few weeks yet, probably just after Christmas. And in the meantime, you can visit her any time you want.''

''Thank you, Shane. I'll give her a good home.''

''I know you will. And I think you'll enjoy her company.''

Tenderly Kelly returned the kitten to its mother. ''Will she miss her mother and brothers when we separate them?''

''For a few days,'' he answered candidly. ''and then you'll take their place.''

Standing, Kelly looked down at the cats again. ''I would take another one to keep her company, but I don't think my little apartment is big enough for two cats.''

''She'll be fine as long as she has you to play with.''

Kelly drew herself away from the cats. ''We'd better get those drinks. Cassie will wonder what's taking us so long.''

Shane led her into his kitchen and opened the refrigerator. He had left a large, wheeled plastic cooler chest waiting to be filled with the extra canned drinks Cassie had asked him to store for her. He and Kelly filled it quickly, and then he closed the cooler and fastened the latch. ''That should hold everyone for the rest of the day.''

Kelly nodded and took a step toward the door. ''Well, then, let's…''

''Kelly, wait.'' He stopped her with a hand on her arm. ''There's something I want to talk to you about.''

Her previously open, relaxed expression changed instantly to vague dismay. He could feel her stiffen beneath his hand, as if she were bracing herself for something. He wondered in exasperation why she was so darned skittish around him lately. Just because he had kissed her once? Had it really been that big a deal for her?

"I overheard some of what you said to Emilio in the barn," he said. "I wasn't deliberately eavesdropping. I didn't realize you were having a personal conversation until it was too late."

Her expression changed to surprise, as if she'd been expecting him to say something else. "I, um..."

When she hesitated, he continued. "What you said to him was really nice. I think it helped put him at ease."

"He seems like a nice boy who's had a difficult time. I hope things work out so he can stay with Lindsay and Nick."

"Nick told me everything looks good so far. He and Lindsay want to keep Emilio until he's eighteen and then help him get into college."

"He's lucky to have found them."

"I want to ask you about something you said to Emilio." Shane chose his words carefully, needing to clarify something that had been bothering him. "Do you really feel like an outsider with us? You told Emilio you're always aware that you aren't really a member of the family. Have we—has anyone in particular made you feel that way?"

Her eyes went wide. "Of course not. Everyone in this family has been incredibly kind to me since the first day I met them. Even before they knew Brynn was Miles's daughter, they took us in and made us welcome."

He wasn't satisfied. "Then you didn't mean what you said to Emilio?"

Kelly hesitated, then shrugged beneath his hand. "Sometimes, on very rare occasions," she emphasized, "I am aware that I have no real connection to the family, neither by blood nor by marriage. It's just an old insecurity, I guess, left over from my childhood. Don't worry about it."

He couldn't let it go that easily. "Kelly, you must know that you're as much a part of this family now as anyone. Most of the kids probably think you are a cousin, and the rest of us never even give it a thought."

"It's okay," she assured him, smiling a little now, her voice soft. "I was only reassuring Emilio that I understand his feelings. I love every member of your family and I'm quite confident that they are genuinely fond of me, too. Don't let my old baggage worry you. As much as I appreciate your concern, I'm really okay with this."

"You're sure?" he asked, searching her face.

"I'm sure." Still smiling, she reached up to touch his cheek. "You can be awfully sweet, you know that?"

The gesture was impulsive, entirely natural, similar to others that had passed between them. A couple of weeks earlier, he might have given her a big, cousinly hug in response, maybe even a friendly kiss. Now he found himself hesitating.

Kelly's eyes locked with his. Her smile faded. Her hand lingered at his cheek, as if she'd momentarily forgotten it was there.

Moving very slowly, he reached up to take her hand in his. He drew it to his lips, and brushed a kiss across her knuckles. Her heard her catch her breath, saw her pupils dilate.

"Shane," she whispered, her voice thin.

She was so pretty. Her mouth so soft. So close. And something about the way she'd said his name just then made his knees go weak. "Kelly," he murmured, and lowered his head, thinking he could give her a little kiss without getting carried away. Just a nice, friendly little…

His mouth settled over hers, and he was lost.

During the past week, Shane had wondered if he'd overreacted to the kiss he and Kelly had shared before. Maybe he'd only imagined that there had been something special about it. Something entirely unexpected. It hadn't really lasted long enough for him to know whether it was different from any other kiss, he had told himself.

This one lasted longer. And he knew immediately that kissing Kelly was not something he could easily dismiss as casual and comfortable.

Kelly didn't immediately draw away. Her mouth softened beneath his, and then moved in a tentative response that was enough to make his head spin. And then her lips parted. Just slightly. Just enough to give him a tantalizing taste of her.

He was suddenly ravenous for more. He wrapped his arms around her and gathered her close, nearly lifting her off her feet as he deepened the kiss. For one delicious moment, Kelly responded with a fervor that seemed to match his.

And then she stiffened and pushed frantically against his shoulders. As reluctant as Shane was to end the kiss, he released her immediately.

She jerked away from him, pressing against the kitchen counter and staring at him with wide, panicky eyes. Her breath came in broken gasps. "Don't," she said. "Don't do that again."

His hand wasn't quite steady when he shoved it

through his hair. "Stop looking so terrified," he said a bit crossly. "I'm not going to attack you."

She swallowed. "Is that the way you treat Dawne when you're alone?"

He'd never heard a more ridiculous question in his life. "Of course not," he snapped. "Damn it, Kelly, Dawne's family."

The silence that followed the comment was heavy with emotion. Her voice was as dark as her unhappy eyes when she finally spoke. "Any more questions about why I sometimes feel like an outsider?"

He swallowed a groan as the full import of what he'd just said sank in. "Kelly, I—"

She didn't give him a chance to finish the stumbling apology. Instead, she turned on one heel and left the room, her limp more pronounced than usual, as if her distress weighed heavily on her. Shane started after her, then stopped with a curse when he remembered the cooler full of drinks. Even with her limp, he couldn't catch up with Kelly while he was dragging a heavy cooler behind him. He was well aware that she would make sure there was no further opportunity for him to talk to her alone that night.

"Walker," he growled to himself, reaching for the cooler handle. "You're an idiot."

There was no one around to dispute him.

Chapter Six

Kelly would never know how she managed, but somehow she made it through the remainder of Thanksgiving evening without anyone seeming to realize that anything was wrong. She smiled, she laughed, she mingled, she ate. She played games. And somehow she avoided looking at Shane. If she had looked at him, her hard-won composure would have shattered for sure.

It was finally time to leave. Kelly was kissed and hugged by seemingly dozens of people—a Walker family tradition. And every kiss reminded her of how much she loved these people, how much it meant to her to be a part of them.

She stood by the door while Brynn and Joe worked the room. Brynn kissed Shane, who'd just kissed three or four aunts and a couple of cousins. "Good night, Brynn," he said.

"Good night, Shane." Brynn hugged him warmly. "Happy Thanksgiving."

Shane shook Joe's hand. "See you next time, Doc."

"Shane, you didn't say good-night to Kelly," Molly, who'd been hovering nearby, reminded him.

"No, I didn't, did I?" Shane sauntered over to Kelly with his usual cowboy grace. He tipped her chin with his hand and leaned over her. "G'night, Kelly. Happy Thanksgiving."

His lips brushed her cheek, setting off an explosion of reaction inside her. And somehow she hid it again behind a bright smile. "Good night, Shane. See you around."

But not for a while, she added silently. Not until they got past whatever was causing this bizarre behavior between them lately.

Kelly considered making an excuse to miss the monthly gathering of her friends, which was to be held at Michael Chang's on the first Friday evening in December. She could tell them she wasn't feeling well. Or that she had other plans. It happened occasionally that someone couldn't make it, and everyone understood.

Amber had called Kelly several times in tearful indecision about whether to attend. Kelly had no idea whether Cameron would make an appearance. She didn't even know if Shane would be there. It depressed her that there were so many problems with the gathering this time. Why couldn't everything have stayed the same as it had been? So easy and comfortable and pleasant. Why had Shane risked ruining their friendship with those impetuous kisses?

She didn't finally decide to go until the afternoon of the party. There were several reasons for her decision.

She didn't want Michael to be hurt if no one showed up. She wanted to be there to support Amber if Amber did decide to attend after all. And, finally, she refused to allow the situation with Shane to keep her away from her friends. Wasn't that exactly what she'd been so afraid of? That a mistake between them would ruin her relationship with their friends and his family?

She didn't know what had gotten into him lately. Why he'd suddenly started looking at her differently. Touching her differently. Kissing her differently.

She should never have sent him those flowers.

There was a knot in the center of her stomach when she rang the doorbell of the small, one-story house Michael had retained after his divorce three years earlier. She hadn't known him when he was married, but Heather had confided that Michael had been heartbroken by the breakup and was still recovering. Kelly had never heard Michael mention his ex-wife.

Was this entire group destined to be unlucky in love? She couldn't help wondering as the door opened and Michael greeted her.

Shane, Scott and Cameron were already gathered in Michael's sparsely furnished living room, munching chips and dip and sipping sodas from frosty bottles. Scott spoke to her first. "Hi, Kelly. Nice sweater."

She'd had the red-and-black striped sweater for a couple of years and knew Scott had seen it before, but he always commented on things like that. "Thanks. Where's Heather?"

"She'll be here. She's just running late—big surprise from my sister, huh?"

Kelly turned then to acknowledge Cameron. "How are you?"

She couldn't quite read his expression when he nodded and murmured, "Hanging in there. How about you?"

"Fine. I read your series of articles last week about the problems at that youth home in Denton. You did a great job with that—very powerful reporting. Have any improvements been made since you exposed the problems?"

He nodded. "There will be a story in tomorrow's edition about the recent changes there, including the hiring of a new director. Only time will tell whether things will really get better, or if the changes are all just public window dressing."

"Will you follow up?"

"Bet on it," he promised. "I'm not so confident that the problems have been solved."

Because she couldn't avoid it any longer, Kelly turned then to greet Shane. "Where's Molly tonight?"

"She's at a sleepover birthday party for a friend. It's something that had been planned for months."

"How has everything been working out with the two of you this week? Any problems?"

"None," he boasted. "We've gotten along just fine. It's been junk food and arcades and movies and go-carts all week. No homework or veggies or curfews. She wants to stay with me forever."

Kelly smiled. "I don't believe a word of that, of course."

Shane made a face. "Okay, maybe we've eaten a veggie or two."

"And maybe Molly's done her homework?"

"Yeah. Maybe. But we really did go to an arcade one afternoon."

"Face it, Shane, you've been Mr. Respectability all

week," Scott teased. "You've probably been more straitlaced with your kid sister than your dad is."

Shane shrugged. "Let's just say I haven't heard her complain."

"Yeah, but she couldn't wait to go to her sleepover party tonight, right?" Cameron ribbed.

"Well…"

"Did you give her the sleepover lecture?" Michael joined in. "Don't leave the house, don't do anything she wouldn't do at home, say 'please' and 'thank you' to the hosts, call you immediately if the other kids start doing anything she knows her parents wouldn't approve of?"

The way Shane shuffled his feet on the carpet let them know that Michael had just come very close to reciting the speech Shane had made to his little sister earlier. "You forgot the part where I reminded her to brush her teeth before bed," he muttered, making the guys laugh and Kelly smile.

The doorbell chimed and Kelly noticed that Cameron's smile faded when Scott commented, "That's probably Heather and Amber."

His guess was correct. Heather came in a bit more vivaciously than usual, chattering rather too spiritedly in an attempt to cover the awkwardness between Amber and Cameron. Amber was noticeably more subdued as she greeted Michael and then Kelly, Scott and Shane. There was palpable pain in her voice when she added quietly, "Hello, Cameron."

"Hi, Amber," he answered gently. "I'm glad you decided to come tonight. It wouldn't have been the same without you."

She gave him a soulful look. "I need my friends."

He winced a little at her tone. "Of course."

And then he turned to start a conversation with Scott about an upcoming college basketball game. Because they couldn't bear to watch Amber watching Cameron, Kelly and Heather swept her into the kitchen on the pretext of making a pot of coffee—something Michael was notoriously bad at.

It wasn't the most comfortable evening the group had ever spent together, but they made it through without tears or shouts, which Kelly decided was a positive sign. Cameron left early, claiming that he had things to do. Amber said very little after he left, but at least she didn't cry. Maybe, with time, everything would get back to normal—between Cameron and Amber, and between Kelly and Shane.

She just wished she could be a little more confident about it.

Molly was to be dropped off by her friend's mother at ten o'clock Saturday morning. Shane had been waiting impatiently for her arrival—so impatiently that it rather amused him. He'd discovered that he was definitely the overprotective type when it came to parenting. He worried constantly about Molly when she was out of his sight, especially since she was his responsibility for now. While he had enjoyed their time together, he would be rather relieved when his parents returned from their vacation and he could turn the reins back over to them.

He wondered if he would worry this much about his own kids. And then he wondered if he would ever have kids to worry about. Shane liked children and had always assumed he would have a family of his own. But kids generally meant a wife, and Shane had yet to meet anyone he'd even considered for that position. As his twenty-eighth birthday drew closer, he couldn't help wondering when—or if—he would ever meet anyone who made him feel the way his father felt about Cassie.

When he heard a car door slam in his driveway, he knew Molly had returned. He waited at the door to greet her with open arms and a big smile. Molly ran through the door, threw her overnight bag on the floor and kept going, straight to the spare bedroom she had been using. Shane caught only a glimpse of her tear-streaked face before she slammed the door closed between them.

After a moment of stunned immobility, he moved quickly to the door. "Molly?"

"Go away," she wailed from the other side. "Please."

"Molly, sweetheart, let's talk about this, okay?" He tried the doorknob, but she had locked it. "Molly?"

"Please, Shane. I just want to be alone, okay? Please just g-go away." The words dissolved then into a torrent of noisy tears.

Shane stared at the blank wooden door in totally baffled dismay. What was he supposed to do now? Pick the lock? Would that really be helpful when she had just begged him to leave her alone?

Another heartrending sob made him rattle the doorknob again. "Molly, open the door. We need to talk."

"No." Misery had turned mutinous now. He had never heard defiance in her voice before.

"Molly, *open the door!*"

"No! Go away, Shane."

Resisting the urge to kick the door in—which, he was sure, was the totally wrong thing to do in this sticky situation—he pushed a hand through his hair and swallowed a curse. He wished his father was here. Jared would have quietly and firmly requested that Molly open the door, and she would have done it. Cassie would have soothed and cajoled her distraught daughter until Molly would have come out to throw herself in her mother's loving arms and spill out whatever it was that was bothering her.

Shane, on the other hand, was clueless about how to handle this. He could leave her alone, as she had requested, but the sound of her crying was ripping him apart. He couldn't just walk away. What he needed, he decided abruptly, was a woman.

He spun on one booted heel and headed for the telephone. Who should he call? One of his aunts? Layla, the tenderhearted, motherly one? Michelle, quiet, gracious, a woman who radiated competence and kindness? Both had daughters of their own, and perhaps some experience with this sort of thing. Or should he call his cousin, Brynn, who had worked in daycare and as a nanny, and was now training to be a schoolteacher? She should know about adolescent traumas, and being closer to Molly's age, she might communicate with her better.

But the number he automatically punched into the keypad belonged to someone else entirely. "Kelly?" he said when she answered on the first ring. "It's Shane. I need help."

It was just over an hour after Shane had called that Kelly parked her car in his driveway and jumped out. She'd arrived as soon as she could get there. She could still hear the echo of the desperation in Shane's voice.

Whatever problems existed between her and Shane, there had been no question about whether she would come when he called to ask for her help. She adored Molly and was as distressed as Shane that something had happened to upset her. She knew it was possible that Shane had managed to deal with the problem while she was on her way, but she was anxious to find out for sure.

Shane had the front door open before she could ring the bell. "Thank you for coming," he said, his tone heartfelt.

He looked, she thought, completely frazzled. His coffee-brown hair was standing straight up in places, as if he'd been dragging his hands through it, and his expression was one of seething frustration.

"Molly still hasn't told you what happened?" Kelly asked.

"She still won't open the door to tell me anything. She stopped crying, I think, but she won't talk. I thought about picking the lock...."

"No, don't do that. Let me try talking to her first. It would be better if it's her decision to let us in."

He waved a hand in the direction of the door. "You're certainly welcome to try."

Kelly took a couple of steps toward the door. Shane was right on her heels. She stopped. "You stay here," she suggested. "I'll call if I need you."

Reluctantly he remained in the living room when she walked down the short hallway to the two bedrooms. The door to Shane's room was standing open, revealing an unmade bed and a bit of masculine clutter. Turning her back on that cozy sight, she knocked on the other door. "Molly?"

The girl sounded startled, her voice still thick with tears. "Who is it?"

"It's Kelly. May I come in?"

"I..." Molly's voice broke, then steadied. "I'm not really in the mood for company right now."

"You're upset. Wouldn't you like someone to talk to?"

There was a long silence, and then a hiccuping sob. "Is Shane out there?"

"Shane's in the living room. It's just us girls, okay?"

Another tense pause, and then the lock clicked on the other side of the door. To Kelly's relief, the door slowly opened. Her relief turned to sympathy when she saw Molly's wet, woebegone face. "Oh, honey, what happened?"

Molly drew her into the room, closed the door again and then burrowed into her arms. "I wish I was dead!"

Kelly winced. It seemed like she'd been hearing that a lot lately. Surely Molly was too young to have had her heart broken.

"Let's sit down and you can tell me about it."

When Molly nodded, Kelly led her to the bed and sat on the edge with her. Holding the girl's cold little hands in hers, she squeezed reassuringly. "Now tell me what's wrong."

Molly bit her full lower lip, looking down at their hands. "Amy Miller and Lacy Dixon made fun of me. They said I have carrot hair and freckles and I don't have any boobs and I'll never have a boyfriend."

Kelly's first reaction was relief that it wasn't a far more serious problem. Her second response was a surge of pure anger. "Why, those snotty little toads!"

Molly was startled into a watery giggle. But her amusement was short-lived. She looked woefully down at her petite, reed-thin body. "They said I look like a boy. They both have figures—Amy's just turned thirteen and she already wears a C-cup. And Lacy's got blond highlights and she's already won two beauty contests."

"She didn't win Miss Congeniality, I bet," Kelly muttered.

Molly looked bewildered. Kelly shook her head. "Never mind. Why did they turn on you that way?"

"I don't know." Molly sniffled. "I was talking to Kristin—she's the one who had the birthday—anyway, I was telling her about the barrel race I won on Sunshine last month, and all of a sudden Amy and Lacy started talking about how many boys they'd kissed and they asked me if I'd ever had a boyfriend and I said no and that's when they told me I probably won't get a boyfriend because boys don't like flat girls with fuzzy red hair and freckles." She stopped for a breath, then added, "Kristin and Patty and Montrieka tried to take up for me, but Amy and Lacy just kept making fun of me until it was time to come home. But I didn't cry in front of them."

"Good for you." Kelly wrapped an arm around Molly's shoulders and hugged. "You listen to me, Molly Walker. Amy and Lacy sound like a couple of bratty bimbos-in-training who don't have the faintest idea what they're talking about. My guess would be that they were jealous of your accomplishments, so they cut you down in a feeble attempt to build themselves up. So Amy's won a couple of beauty contests…"

"Lacy," Molly corrected.

"Whatever. Big deal. She knows how to walk down a runway in an expensive dress without falling on her face. She also knows that isn't nearly as challenging and exciting as the competitive riding you do. I've seen you ride, remember? And Molly, you are pure poetry on horseback. You're so beautiful when you fly around those barrels that it takes my breath away."

Molly looked hopeful. "Really?"

"Absolutely. And your hair is lovely. The color of a fiery sunset. You look exactly like your mother."

"My mother's pretty," Molly whispered.

Kelly smiled. "Yes, she is. You only have to ask your dad to know that. I bet he thinks she's the most beautiful woman he's ever seen."

Molly seemed somewhat encouraged, but not entirely convinced. "Cameron calls me gorgeous sometimes," she murmured.

"Well, there you go. If anyone should know a pretty girl when he sees one, it's Cameron."

"I'm still flat."

"So was I, at your age," Kelly confided. She wrinkled her nose. "I still don't wear a C-cup. I've had to settle for a B."

"You have a great figure, Kelly. And you're so pretty."

Giving the girl another hug, Kelly smiled again. "Thank you, sweetie. But believe me, I went through my gawky stage—all knees and elbows and ears and teeth. Why do you think I wear my hair so short?"

"I thought you just like it short."

"Yes—but mostly because it's straight as a stick. I can't do a thing with it when it gets too long. I used to dream about having soft, natural curls like yours."

Molly lifted a hand slowly to her tousled hair. "You did?"

"Absolutely. You are as pretty as any girl I know. And you're so much *more* than pretty—smart and funny and loving and talented, all of which are more valuable than outward appearance. When the time is right for you to have a boyfriend, the boys will notice you. In the meantime, you have a great time and don't let anyone put you down. Next time they try, hold your chin up and tell them you are perfectly happy with your looks and your life and you wouldn't trade places with them—or anyone.''

"Okay, I will."

"And if that doesn't work, tell me and I'll go give them a piece of my mind."

Molly smiled weakly and leaned her head on Kelly's shoulder. "They really hurt my feelings."

"I know, baby. I'm sorry."

"I won't let them do that to me again."

"No." Kelly hoped Molly would talk about this incident with her parents, who would probably know better than Kelly what their child needed to hear. "Molly—Shane's really worried about you. You think we should go talk to him?"

Molly made a face. "Is he mad at me?"

"Why would he be mad at you?"

"Because I wouldn't talk to him. I—I didn't think he would understand. He's… Well, he's a guy. And he's my brother. He doesn't want me to have a boyfriend anyway."

Kelly couldn't help smiling. "Not for a few more years, I'm sure."

Mopping her face with her hand, Molly swallowed. "A bunch of girls are already going out with guys. That's all they talk about. But I don't want to do that right now, Kelly. I just want to hang out with my friends and ride my horses and do things with my family, you know?"

"I know." She pulled a clean tissue out of her pocket and dried Molly's cheeks. "And there's nothing at all wrong with that."

"Lacy said it's weird not to have a boyfriend."

"Hmm. Do you think *I'm* weird, Molly?"

The child's eyes rounded. "Of course not! You're one of the coolest people I know."

"Thank you. But I don't have a boyfriend."

"You don't?"

"No. I have a lot of friends who happen to be guys, and I enjoy their company very much. But I'm not really looking for a boyfriend until I finish college and get a job. Like you, I'm just not ready for a boyfriend right now."

"Does anyone ever tease you about it?" Molly asked a bit shyly.

"If they ask, I tell them I'm waiting for someone very special, and I'm not willing to settle for just anyone— unlike *some* desperate girls who think they need a boyfriend to make them cool."

Molly's eyebrows rose. "I think a girl can be cool without a boyfriend. Like you. And Dawne—she hasn't had a boyfriend since she broke up with jerky Jordan last year—that's what she calls him now anyway."

"See? Dawne wasn't going to settle, either. She knows she deserves someone special, and she's willing to wait for him. You have plenty of time in the future for boyfriends and romance, sweetie. But you only get to be twelve years old for a little while. It's a great age— don't let anyone take the fun away from you."

Impulsively Molly reached up to kiss Kelly's cheek. "Thank you."

"You're welcome." Kelly cleared her throat. "Now wash your face and comb your pretty red hair and let's go put poor Shane out of his misery, okay?"

"Okay." Molly dashed toward the tiny adjoining bathroom and a moment later, Kelly heard water running.

She spent the brief time she waited imagining ways

to take revenge on a couple of catty adolescent girls. Glue in their hair gel? Food dye in their makeup? Ants in their C-cups? She would never follow up on those ignoble fantasies, of course, but it gave her a grim satisfaction to imagine retribution for Molly's humiliation.

Molly returned with a rosy face and a sweet smile that made all her negative thoughts vanish. She stood and held out her hand. "Let's go see Shane."

Chapter Seven

They found Shane pacing the living room, his hands in his hair again. He spun to look at them when he heard them approach. Kelly and Molly smiled at him.

"I'm hungry, Shane," Molly announced. "When's lunch?"

Shane stared at her. "Er...are you okay?"

"I'm fine. Kelly made me feel better. Have you fed my guinea pig today?"

"No. The cage is still in the laundry room."

"Okay. I'll go feed him." Molly spun and moved toward the laundry room at her usual pace—top speed.

Shane watched his little sister out of sight and then turned slowly to Kelly. "What on earth did you say to her?"

"Girl talk," she answered breezily. "She's fine, Shane. Don't worry about her, okay?"

"Don't *worry?* She spent an hour in her room, crying

as if her heart was broken, and I'm just supposed to forget about it?''

"A couple of snotty brats hurt her feelings at the party. I'm not going to tell you what they said because I don't think Molly would want me to, but she and I talked about it and I don't think she'll let them hurt her again.''

"They'd damned well better not," Shane growled, his eyes flashing. "Tell me their names and I'll call their parents. And then I'm calling Kristin's mother and asking what she was thinking, letting a child be attacked in her home.''

"You aren't calling anyone," Kelly replied firmly. "The only purpose that would serve is to give the brats more ammunition to use against her. Let Molly try to handle this. If she decides she wants your help, she'll ask for it.''

He blew out an impatient breath. "Darn it, I want to pound someone for making her cry.''

"So do I—but you really can't pound a couple of teenage girls.''

Shane muttered something incomprehensible.

"She'll probably tell Cassie about it. Cassie will know exactly what to say to make her feel better," Kelly predicted confidently.

"Apparently you did, too. She went into that room sobbing and she came out smiling.''

She could tell from Shane's expression that he was a bit hurt that Molly hadn't been able to talk to him. She laid a hand on his arm. "She really just wanted a woman's perspective on this one. She knows you'll always be there for her when she needs you.''

"So what about lunch, Shane?" Molly asked, bouncing back into the room. "Can Kelly eat with us?''

Shane ruffled Molly's freshly brushed hair and smiled at Kelly. "I'd like that. Kelly, will you have lunch with us? We thought we'd go out to eat today."

"Well, I..."

"Please, Kelly," Molly said winningly. "First you can visit the kitten Shane's giving you when she's old enough to leave her mother, and then we'll all go out to eat. It will be fun."

She couldn't refuse. "I would love to join you for lunch. Thank you."

Beaming, Molly caught Kelly's hand in her right hand and Shane's in her left. "This is going to be great."

Kelly's eyes met Shane's. And something in his expression made her swallow hard.

"Yeah," he said quietly, speaking to Molly but still looking at Kelly. "This is going to be great."

Shane and Kelly allowed Molly to select the restaurant for lunch. Hardly to Shane's surprise, she chose her favorite Tex-Mex place, which was attached to a shopping center just outside of Dallas. The mall was crowded with Saturday-afternoon Christmas shoppers, and glittering with decorations. Even though they were a bit early for the lunch rush, they had to wait fifteen minutes for a table. Molly didn't seem to mind.

"This place has the most awesome nachos," she assured Kelly. "But the other food is good, too."

Kelly promised to keep that in mind.

When they were finally seated, Shane ordered an appetizer of raw vegetables and dip—to make the fast-food meal more nutritious, he assured them gravely—and fruit punch all around. He chuckled when a man dressed as Santa Claus in a sombrero passed their table playing "Feliz Navidad" on a guitar. "Molly and I like only the most elegant restaurants,'' he assured Kelly as two squealing children dashed past their table in the singing Santa's wake.

''This place is fun,'' she assured him with a smile.

He should have known Kelly would enjoy this noisy mall eatery as much as an elegant restaurant. He had always liked her naturally unpretentious manner. Watching as she chatted with Molly, he admired the way the twinkling, multicolored Christmas lights reflected in her fair hair and sparkling eyes. She looked like a Christmas sprite, he thought fancifully. Her green-and-gold sweater added to the illusion. It occurred to him that he wouldn't mind finding her under his tree on Christmas morning.

He realized abruptly that his feelings for Kelly had undergone a radical change in the last few weeks. He wasn't even trying now to convince himself that he thought of Kelly exactly the same way he thought of his cousins. He knew she wouldn't want to hear that—she'd made that perfectly clear when he had kissed her on Thanksgiving—but somehow it had happened.

Now he wasn't sure exactly what to do about it.

She glanced his way, saw him watching her, flushed a little and quickly turned back to Molly. And Shane was left to consider the possibility that Kelly didn't think of him quite as a cousin, either.

Shane was staring at her again. Kelly glanced at him from beneath her lashes as they finished their meal with fried ice cream for dessert—another of Molly's suggestions. She looked quickly down again after confirming her suspicion that Shane was watching her.

She wished she knew what was going through his mind.

"Can we walk around the mall for a little while after lunch?" Molly asked eagerly.

Though Kelly knew shopping wasn't one of Shane's favorite pastimes, she wasn't surprised when he agreed. He didn't refuse Molly very often, and after her upset earlier, he was in a particularly indulgent mood.

Molly seemed to have almost forgotten about her earlier distress. Whether because Kelly's words had meant something to her, or because she was enjoying this outing—or whether her adolescent hormones had simply settled down for a while—Molly was in a particularly sunny mood now. She seemed enthralled by all the Christmas displays, and couldn't seem to take it all in fast enough as she craned her head from side to side, looking at everything and everyone around them.

Molly was much too old to visit Santa Claus, of course, but Kelly saw her smile and wave at the bearded guy, who gave her a friendly wave in return. Molly lingered for a few minutes in front of display of new CDs, but politely declined Shane's offer to buy her one. "I have CDs on my Christmas list," she explained. And then her face lit up again. "Hey, there's an arcade!"

Minutes later, Shane, Molly and Kelly were lined up in front of Skeeball games, trying to roll their wooden balls into the high-score slots. Molly and Shane had a fierce competition going, bragging noisily about their Skeeball skills and predicting victory in the points battle. Both seemed surprised when Kelly ended the game with the highest score and the greatest number of prize tickets.

"Way to go, Kelly," Molly said, laughing at the startled look on her brother's face. "You beat Shane—and he thinks he's the Skeeball champ."

"I demand a rematch," Shane declared, plugging another token into his machine. "I was blindsided."

She smiled sweetly at him and inserted her own token. As the wooden balls clattered noisily into the chute, she murmured, "Let's just see who's the real Skeeball champ."

Shane's eyes lit with the fire of competition. Molly clapped her hands and cheered Kelly on, choosing to watch rather than play this time. And at the end of nine rolls, Kelly once again had the high score.

As Molly laughed in delight, Shane planted his fists on his hips and studied Kelly with narrowed eyes. "So how are you at shooting targets with Ping-Pong ball guns?" he demanded, motioning toward another game.

"Adequate," she replied vaguely, and pushed the sleeves of her sweater higher on her arms.

She soon proved she was more than adequate. Ping-Pong balls whooshed steadily out of her air-powered "gun," and stuffed targets fell swiftly, one by one. When the game ended, she had tied Shane twice and beaten him once. Handing the prize tickets to Molly, Shane challenged, "Let's see how good you are at air hockey."

She soon showed him that she was *very* good at air hockey. As the plastic puck shot past his paddle to clatter into the goal slot, she straightened and absently brushed her hair out of her eyes. "Seven to five," she announced unnecessarily. "I win."

"Okay," Shane growled, moving to stand toe-to-toe with her, "how did you get so good at arcade games?"

She laughed. "I worked at one of those pizza-and-prizes places when I was in high school. After work, the employees would spend an hour or so playing the arcade games, on the pretext of making sure everything was working properly. After working there for two years, I was named the arcade queen.''

"You might have told me that *before* you accepted my challenges,'' Shane muttered.

Her smile widened. "And miss seeing you bust a gut trying to beat me?''

Molly giggled. "She got you good, Shane.''

"Yes,'' he agreed, his mouth quirking into his attractively crooked smile. "She got me good.''

Kelly tugged at the high collar of her sweater and looked away. "Does it seem warm in here to either of you? Hey, Molly, do you want to try the claw machine? Maybe we can make it pick up a stuffed animal.''

Easily distracted, Molly headed for the game, her attention already focused on a small teddy bear on top of the rather tightly packed pile of prizes. "Kelly,'' Shane said when she started after his sister.

She paused. "Yes?''

"Next time, we'll choose a game *I* can win.''

Because she had a nagging suspicion he wasn't talking about arcade games, she cleared her throat and then hurried over to Molly without coming up with anything to say in reply.

They were leaving the arcade, Molly carrying two stuffed-animal prizes, when they heard someone hail them. "What are you guys doing here?'' Keith Samples asked as he entered the arcade.

"Hi, Keith. Do you like arcades, too?'' Molly greeted her college-freshman cousin.

"Yeah, they're cool.'' Keith motioned idly to the two fashionably shaggy young men who accompanied him. "These are my friends, Bodie and Matt. Guys, meet my cousins, Molly, Shane and Kelly.''

"Hey,'' the guys grunted in unison.

"It's nice to meet you," Kelly said, aware that Keith had made no distinction between his relationship with her and the Walker siblings.

Maybe Shane was right, she thought as the two groups parted again. Maybe the younger generation *had* accepted her as a cousin when they'd taken in Brynn. Maybe they all thought of her simply as family.

All except Shane, of course, she added, remembering kisses that hadn't been at all familial. She wasn't sure how Shane thought of her now.

She wasn't even sure how she thought of *him*.

They were headed toward the mall exit when Molly pointed to the multiplex movie theater located on the lower level. "They have that Christmas movie I've been wanting to see," she hinted broadly, gazing up at Shane.

Shane looked from Molly to the theater marquis, and then to Kelly. "Kelly might have other plans for the rest of the day," he suggested.

Molly's soulful eyes turned immediately toward Kelly.

Molly had been having such a good time on their outing. Kelly couldn't bring herself to put an end to it just yet. So maybe she and Shane were shamelessly spoiling the girl today; how could they not after those miserable tears earlier? "Actually, I've been wanting to see that movie myself," she fibbed. "And I have nothing better to do this afternoon," she added, mentally dismissing the rather lengthy list of chores she had planned to tackle on this rare day off.

"Great," Molly said, breaking away from them. "I'll go see when the next feature starts."

"Liar," Shane murmured to Kelly.

She kept her eyes on Molly. "I don't mind. Really."

"If there are other things you need to do, I can take Molly to see the movie another time."

"No. I can spare another couple of hours for her."

"Have I told you how much I appreciate what you've done for her today?"

She waved a hand dismissively. "I've had a good time, too."

It wasn't long before the movie started. They passed that time having sodas in the food court. When they filed into the theater row, they put Molly between them, but when the film began, she whispered that she couldn't see over the man in front of her. A little shuffling resulted in Shane sitting in the middle, Molly on his left and Kelly at his right. And then the theater went dark and the film began and Kelly tried to concentrate on the plot rather than the way Shane's shoulder touched hers in the crowded row. He shifted in his seat and his thigh brushed hers. Her spine almost melted.

By the time the movie ended, she wasn't sure she could have summarized the plot if anyone asked her. But she could probably give the exact number of times Shane had touched her, either accidentally or on purpose. She could have described every time he glanced at her in the pale light filtering from the movie screen. And she could have named the exact moment when she realized in despair that there seemed to be no going back to the comfortably friendly relationship they had before Shane kissed her.

She knew she was quiet on the way back to the ranch. Fortunately Molly chattered so much that Kelly's near silence wasn't overly noticeable. The telephone was ringing when they walked through Shane's door. He snatched it up before the machine could answer. A moment later, he looked at his sister. "It's for you," he said. "It's Kristin."

Molly took the phone. "Hi, Kristin. Sure, I'm fine. I've had a really fun day with my brother and our friend. Oh, no, I didn't let Amy and Lacy bother me," she said airily. "If they don't like me, that's their problem, not mine." She grinned and gave Kelly a thumbs-up, which Kelly proudly returned.

Shane motioned Kelly into the kitchen, leaving Molly to babble on about every detail of her day.

"I'd better be going," Kelly said, glancing at her watch the moment she and Shane were alone. "I still have an hour's drive ahead of me."

"Kelly, you and I need to talk."

She took a step toward the door, having no need to ask what he wanted to talk about. "We've already talked. It's all settled now. There's no need to bring it up again."

"I don't think we've settled anything," he replied, taking two steps toward her. "There are still some issues we should discuss."

She eyed him warily. "I don't see any need to rehash a couple of mistakes. It's not as if it's going to happen again."

"Won't it?" Another step brought Shane to within a foot of her. "Are you so sure about that?"

She pushed her hands in her pockets and lifted her chin in a show of bravado. "I'm sure. Neither of us wants to risk—"

"Don't speak for me, Kelly."

She blinked in surprise at his uncharacteristically curt tone. "I'm not...."

"I want to kiss you again. Right now, as a matter of fact."

She looked quickly toward the kitchen doorway, relieved that Molly was still on the phone in the other room. "Shane, please."

"Please what? Please pretend that nothing happened? Please lie about the way I feel? I'm afraid I can't do that anymore."

"We can't talk about this now," she whispered, worried that Molly would overhear.

"No," he agreed. "Not now. But soon."

"I…"

"Hey, guys, guess what?" Molly skipped through the door in cheerful obliviousness to the tension between the adults. "Kristin told Amy and Lacy that she thought they were real jerks to me, and if they ever say anything like that again, she's going to tell everyone at school that they're jealous losers. Kristin thinks they're going to apologize to me tomorrow."

"And you will accept their apologies very graciously," Kelly instructed. "That makes you look even more superior to them."

Molly smiled. "Then that's exactly what I'll do."

Turning away from Kelly, Shane once again demonstrated his ability to completely mask his emotions. "If those girls start in on you again, tell me and I'll pound them for you," he offered, his tone only half-teasing.

Molly giggled. "No, you wouldn't. But thanks for offering."

Kelly took advantage of the opportunity to escape while Molly was there to distract Shane. Molly tried to talk her into staying a little longer, but Kelly was able to convince her that she really had to go. "Just remember everything I told you earlier, okay?"

Molly smiled and gave her a hug. "I'll remember. Bye, Kelly. Thanks for everything."

"You're welcome, sweetie." She paused. "Goodbye, Shane."

"Drive carefully."

"Yes, I will." She left quickly, escaping to her car. She turned the radio up to a high volume during the drive home in a futile attempt to drown out her painful thoughts.

One question was uppermost in her mind during that drive—and the near sleepless night that followed. *Why had Shane ruined everything?*

When someone rang Kelly's doorbell later that week, she briefly considered not answering. She had her last semester final the next day, and she had been studying for hours—both because she wanted to do well on the test and because she wanted to distract herself from thoughts of Shane. She was afraid she would find him on the other side of her door, and she didn't know if she was up to another disturbing confrontation.

The doorbell rang again and she sighed. Giving in to the inevitable, she forced herself to move to the door and check the peephole.

It wasn't Shane on her doorstep. She blinked in surprise as she realized that it was one of his uncles instead. She opened the door slowly, trying to put a name to him. After more than a year of socializing with them at Walker family gatherings, Kelly still had a hard time telling the twins apart. They were identical, both lean and handsome in their early forties, with golden-brown hair and light blue eyes that could change instantly from warm to frosty. One of them—Ryan, she believed—had a faint, faded scar at his right temple from an old accident. Seeing no scar now, she hazarded, "Joe?"

He nodded, smiling faintly. His manner, too, helped

her identify him. Joe Walker was the more serious-natured twin, Ryan the more ebullient. Kelly probably hadn't exchanged more than two dozen words with Joe since she'd met him. All she really knew about him was that he, like his twin, worked for Tony D'Alessandro's private investigation agency, and that he adored his accountant wife, Lauren, and their ten-year-old son, Casey.

She couldn't imagine why Joe Walker was calling on her at six o'clock on a Thursday evening, but she smiled and opened the door wider. "Please, come in."

He was carrying a leather portfolio, she noted as he passed her into the living room. It made the visit seem more official somehow. "Can I get you anything?" she asked. "Coffee?"

He declined politely. "I need to talk to you about something."

Trying futilely to guess what he might want to talk to her about, she motioned toward the couch. "Please, sit down."

He settled on the end of the couch, setting the leather portfolio on the table in front of him. Kelly perched on a nearby chair. "What is this about, Joe?"

Opening the folder, he extracted a five-by-seven-inch photograph. "Do you recognize this man?"

The uniformed man in the picture was older than she remembered, his hair a bit grayer, his face somewhat more lined. But she knew him immediately from photographs her mother had left her. "This is my father, air force colonel Jack Morrison. The last I heard, he was stationed somewhere in Europe."

Joe nodded. "I wondered if you would recognize the photograph."

"Has something happened to him?" Was *that* what this visit was about? Was she being officially notified, as her father's heir, perhaps, that she was now an orphan in reality, though she had been virtually orphaned when her mother died over ten years ago?

"No, he's fine," Joe assured her. "He's looking for you actually. He wants to see you again, and he doesn't know where you've been living since you moved from Longview."

Kelly blinked in surprise. "You're kidding," she said blankly—her first reaction to the unexpected news.

"I'm not known for being much of a kidder."

Despite her confusion, she couldn't help smiling a little at his wry tone. She had always liked Joe Walker, even though she didn't know him well. And then her smile faded. "How do you know he's looking for me?"

"He contacted our agency, which isn't so surprising, considering that we've earned a reputation in this state for reuniting families. I happened to take the call."

"Did you tell him where I am?"

"I didn't even tell him I know you," Joe replied. "I told him I would look into it and get back to him."

"I can't believe he wants to see me again after all these years." She pressed her fingertips to her suddenly throbbing temples. "The last time I saw him, I was eight years old. I didn't even hear from him when my mother died. Do you know about my mother, Joe?"

"Why don't you tell me about her?"

"She was German. My father met her when he was stationed at Spangdahlem Air Base twenty-five years ago. He married her, brought her to Marshall, Texas— his hometown—and then spent most of their marriage away from her. My father was on temporary assignment in the Philippines when I was born. He thought his family in Marshall would look out for his wife, but they didn't like her. His father was a World War II veteran who was vehemently opposed to having a German daughter-in-law. My parents stayed married for seven years, and then he divorced her, leaving her to raise their child alone in this new country.''

She sighed heavily, the memories weighing on her. ''I saw my father one time after the divorce. He popped in for a visit on my eighth birthday. He brought me a shiny new bicycle, patted me on the head and then vanished from my life again. He sent monthly support checks— probably an automatic deduction from his paycheck. My mother banked them for my education, moving to Longview and working two jobs there to support me. When I was eleven, she developed cancer. She couldn't take care of me, so she placed me in a foster home run by Ethel Fendel, a friend of hers. That's where I met Brynn. Two years later, after a long, painful illness, my mother died. My father's monthly checks continued to be deposited into my trust fund, but I never heard from him. Not a call, not a card. Nothing. And now he wants to see me again?''

''You don't have to see him, Kelly. I can tell him I contacted you, and you requested that he respect your privacy and leave you alone.''

Kelly twisted her fingers in her lap. ''That's what I *should* do, isn't it?''

''I didn't say that.''

She studied his unrevealing face. ''You think I should see him?''

''I didn't say that, either.'' Joe rested his forearms on his knees, leaning toward her. ''This is entirely your decision. There is no right or wrong choice, only what feels right to you.''

''Oh, you're a lot of help.'' She gave him a wry smile.

He returned it ruefully. ''Sorry. I'm afraid I'm not

very good at that sort of thing. But if it helps, I can understand how you feel—at least a little. When I learned that my brother and sisters were looking for me after more than twenty years apart, I wasn't at all certain I wanted to see them again. Ryan and I had made a pretty good life for ourselves, and I wasn't sure I wanted the complication of a family I hardly remembered.''

''What changed your mind?''

''Lauren,'' he admitted. ''And Ryan. Both of them were curious about the family, and both thought we needed to put the past to rest in order to get on with our futures.''

''I don't have to ask how the reunion turned out. You seem happy to have your family back in your life.''

''I am,'' he answered simply.

''But you have to admit this is different. You and your siblings were separated through no fault of your own. My father chose to leave. He chose to let me be raised in a foster home. He could have been there for me when I needed him, but he wasn't.''

Joe nodded gravely. ''No one could blame you if you don't want to see him again.''

Kelly looked at the photograph again. She might have recognized the face, but she didn't know this man. He hadn't been a father to her when she had needed a father. Now that she was a self-sufficient adult, what role could he possibly play in her life? ''I really need to think about this before I make a decision.''

''Of course you do.'' Joe stood, his business concluded. ''I'll let him know that you've been notified and that you've requested time. You take as long as you want.''

She walked him to the door. ''Thank you for handling

this so considerately, Joe. I appreciate the way you've respected my privacy.''

He nodded. ''You've become a part of my family during the past couple of years. I watch out for my family.''

His gruffly spoken words touched her. Family, she thought, had little to do with blood, and everything to do with feelings. ''Thank you.''

''Call me when you decide what you want to do.''

''I will.'' She reached out to open the door for him. ''I'll let you know as soon as I...''

Her voice died away when she opened the door to find Shane on the doorstep, his finger poised above the doorbell. He looked as surprised as she felt.

''Joe,'' he said, staring at his uncle with narrowed eyes. ''What the hell are you doing here?''

Chapter Eight

Rather than answering Shane's question, Joe greeted his nephew. "Hello, Shane. I heard your folks got back from their vacation yesterday. Did they have a good time?"

"Yeah, they had a great time," Shane answered absently, studying the portfolio Joe carried beneath one arm. "Was this a business or social call?"

Joe smiled. "You always were a curious kid. I would have thought you'd have outgrown it by now."

He glanced then at Kelly. "I'll leave you to deal with your pal's questions."

Great, she thought as Joe and Shane passed in her doorway, Shane without waiting for an invitation to enter. As if the evening hadn't been stressful enough.

Shane turned in the middle of the living room floor to look at her. "What did Joe want?"

She closed the door in a mixture of resignation and

irritation. "Has it occurred to you that it's absolutely none of your business?"

"I just want to know if something is wrong," he insisted. "My uncle was obviously in P.I. mode, so either you've hired him for some reason…"

Kelly rolled her eyes. "Why would I hire a private investigator?"

"Then he was here because he's come across something that concerns you."

She knew Shane wouldn't be satisfied until he found out what was going on. Had she really been opposed to telling him, she would have firmly repeated that it was none of his business and asked him to leave. And he would have gone—albeit reluctantly. But the truth was, this was exactly the sort of thing she would have wanted to discuss with Shane when she had thought of him simply as one of her best friends.

She needed that friend now.

"Your uncle was here on behalf of my father. Apparently, D'Alessandro Investigations has earned a reputation for reuniting long-separated family members. I didn't bother to leave a forwarding address when I moved here eighteen months ago—I didn't know there was anyone who would want to contact me—so my father hired Joe to find me."

Shane rubbed the back of his neck, looking thoughtful, but not particularly surprised. "How long has it been since you saw your father?"

"Sixteen years. I was eight. I haven't heard a word from him since."

Shane had spotted the photograph still lying on her coffee table. He picked it up and studied it. "You have his eyes."

Kelly pushed a hand through the fair hair she'd inherited from her mother. "I know."

He looked at her over the photograph. "Do you want to talk about it?"

"Do I have a choice?" she asked wryly.

He frowned. "You know you do. If you want me to leave, say so."

She sighed. "Don't go."

The truth was, she didn't want to be alone with her memories right now. And Shane was one of the few people she would have wished for had she been by herself tonight. "Sit down," she said. "We'll talk."

He sat on the same end of the couch his uncle had just vacated. Kelly automatically started to sit beside him, then hesitated and moved toward a chair instead.

"Damn it, get back over here," he growled crossly. "We can't talk with you way over there. Stop acting like I'm going to jump you or something."

Her cheeks warming, she perched on the opposite end of the couch. "Don't be ridiculous," she muttered, feeling as irritable as he sounded.

He cleared his throat and spoke in a more amicable tone. "Are you going to meet with your father?"

"I asked Joe to give me some time to think about it. He said he understood, and he thought I should take as much time as I need."

"Of course Joe understands. He's been through this himself."

"I know. He told me a little about it."

"He obviously likes you. Joe isn't one to talk about himself much."

"I like him, too. He's so…steady." That was what made him such a good husband and father, she thought.

Kelly couldn't imagine any circumstance that would pull Joe Walker away from his wife and son.

Shane smiled. "That's a good word for him. Not the first word that would come to mind about his twin, but it describes Joe perfectly."

She was well aware that happy-go-lucky Ryan Walker was as loyal to his wife and sons as his brother was to his family. The Walker twins would never voluntarily abandon their children, she was certain—and neither would Jared, or Nick, or Tony or Joe D'Alessandro, or any of the other admirable men she had come to know through this family. Which made it all the more difficult for her to understand her own father's actions.

"So are you going to see him?"

She twisted her fingers in her lap. "I don't know."

"I'm sure you're angry with him."

Frowning, she gave the comment some thought. "I used to be. But now...I don't know."

"It's okay if you are. I know I was mad at my mother."

Struck by his tone, she turned a bit more to face him. "Are you still?"

"Of course. She didn't abandon me physically, the way your father did you, but every time she picked up a bottle of booze, she might as well have been in another country for all the attention she paid me."

"Your father was in the service when you were young, wasn't he?"

"Yes. The navy."

"And he was gone a lot, leaving you alone with your mother?"

Shane didn't seem to like that question. "Dad was on sea duty a lot when I was a kid, but he had to make a living. He tried to get custody of me when he and my mother divorced, but the courts weren't very progressive about such things then. He sent me letters and gifts and he called when he could, and between tours he spent every free minute with me.''

''I'm not criticizing Jared,'' she said quickly, conciliatorily. ''You know I'm very fond of him, and I think he's a wonderful father to you and Molly. I just wondered…well, did you ever get mad at him for not being there more often? For leaving you to be neglected by an alcoholic mother and her husband?''

Shane shook his head. ''My dad did the best he could. And when I ran away to find him—when he realized how bad things had gotten for me at home—he got out of the navy to take care of me. He worked his butt off to support me the next few years until he could make arrangements to buy the ranch.''

''So you were never angry at him during those unhappy years?''

''Never,'' he assured her, though the answer, at least in her opinion, lacked his usual conviction.

''You never blamed him—even the tiniest bit—for going off to sea while you were so miserable in your home? For not recognizing sooner how unhappy you were?''

''Look, we're supposed to be talking about your feelings for *your* father,'' Shane said abruptly, determinedly changing the subject. ''Yours is the one waiting for an answer about whether you want to see him again.''

Why was Shane so reluctant to talk about his deepest emotions—especially when he never hesitated to inquire about hers? Kelly had thought they'd made a step toward an intimacy of sorts the night he'd told her about his mother's death. Apparently she'd been wrong. Shane's emotional baggage, if he had any, was well hidden once again.

"Fine," she said a bit shortly, refusing to analyze why she was both disappointed and hurt by his reticence with her. "There's really nothing more to say about my father. He disappeared and now he's back. And I need some time to think about whether I have any interest in seeing him again."

"Seeing him might make it easier for you to resolve the past. It would give you a chance to ask him why he left you. Why he never tried to contact you."

"You said you went to see your mother a couple of years ago. Did seeing her again help you resolve *your* past?"

If he felt any pain at the mention of his unsuccessful last meeting with his late mother, he didn't let it show. "My mother was too drunk when I saw her to answer any questions about anything. And there's another difference—I was the one who initiated the meeting. She didn't care if she never saw me again. Your father is the one making this effort."

She nodded somberly. "But it may just be too late."

"That's for you to decide, of course. Just—don't burn any bridges."

"I haven't even struck a match yet," she assured him. "I just don't want to rush into a reunion without deciding first how I feel and what I want to say."

"Perfectly understandable."

"I'm glad you approve," she responded wryly.

The irony seemed to sail right over his handsome head. "When did you tell Joe you'd give him an answer?"

"We left it open."

"If you want my advice—"

"I'll ask for it," she cut in firmly. "Thank you, but this is something I have to decide for myself."

"Kelly." Shane reached out to cover her hand with his. "Do you *want* to see your father again?"

She looked at him without trying to hide her tangled emotions. "When I was a little girl, I used to pray every time the doorbell rang that my father would be on the other side of the door. When I was eleven and my mother got sick, I was sure my father would come home and make everything better. And when she died, I fantasized that he would come take me to live with him—and that he would adopt Brynn while he was at it, so I would always have her for my sister."

Shane wrapped an arm loosely around her shoulders, the gesture so natural, so like the "old" Shane, that she didn't even think about pulling away. "When did you stop hoping he would come back?"

"The night of my high school graduation. For some really stupid reason, I thought he would be there. I don't know why, since I didn't mail him an invitation—I didn't know where to send it—but I thought he would know. I looked for him all evening. The only person who snapped my picture when I accepted my diploma was Brynn. I decided right then that she was the only family I needed."

Shane rested his cheek against her hair. "He really hurt you badly. No one would blame you if you never wanted to see him again."

"That's what Joe said."

"I agree with him."

She let out a long, weary breath, her thoughts focused on her father's unexpected reemergence. She savored the warmth of Shane's arm around her, the comfort of his loyal support. She had a new family now, she thought with a touch of defiance. She didn't need her father. Why should she subject herself to emotional distress just to ease his conscience—or whatever he wanted from this reunion?

"Whatever you want," Shane said, "whatever makes you happy—that's what I want you to do. Your father was an idiot to stay away from you. He doesn't deserve a daughter like you."

She tilted her head to smile up at him. "That was just what I needed to hear. Thank you."

He rested a hand against her cheek. "You're welcome."

And it happened again. Their gazes locked. The air seemed to crackle around them, as if suddenly filled with static electricity. She was in Shane's arms and suddenly it was not a safe, comfortable place to be.

She started to draw away. Shane's arm tightened, holding her in place. "Don't go away," he murmured. "This is nice."

Nice? It was entirely too risky. This could all too easily lead to kissing again—and she certainly didn't want *that* to happen.

But it did. And when Shane's mouth came down on hers, she did absolutely nothing to stop him.

Maybe it was the strain of hearing about her father that made her seek comfort in Shane's embrace. Perhaps she thought they might as well get this behind them, since it had been inevitable. Maybe if they could just satisfy their curiosity or whatever it was that had been initiating these kisses, they would be able to get past this new, unwelcome awkwardness between them and get back to the way they had been before.

The kiss probably wouldn't even be as spectacular as

she'd remembered, she thought as she allowed her lips to soften beneath his.

Shane's left arm was still wrapped around her shoulders. His right hand rested against her cheek. She sank into him, her lips parting slightly—just enough to allow him to promptly take advantage and deepen the kiss.

Shane drew her closer, moving slowly, giving her every opportunity to pull away. She made no effort to do so, telling herself she was merely trying to prove her new theory that it had been her resistance, her panic, that had made the previous kisses seem so exciting. So dangerous. She told herself it would be different this time. They would determine once and for all that kissing each other was no big deal, hardly worth the risk of ruining their previously uncomplicated relationship.

She told herself those things even as her arms closed around his neck. Even as she pressed more tightly against him. Even as his tongue swept past her lips to explore every inch of her mouth. *No big deal,* she reminded herself, even as her blood ran hotter and her heart began to race.

Shane shifted on the couch, leaning over her, pressing her into the deep cushions behind her. He changed the angle of the kiss, his lips moving hotly, hungrily over hers, his tongue probing, tasting, savoring.

Just a kiss, she reminded herself even as her fingers burrowed into his crisp, thick hair, holding him closer.

And then his hand slid slowly down her side to pause at her hip, to fit her more snugly against him. And her entire body reacted with an explosion of sensation so intense, so needy that it terrified her.

She ripped her mouth from beneath his. "Shane, stop."

He froze, hesitating only a moment before reluctantly pulling away. "Too fast?" he asked, his voice husky.

"Too *everything*," she answered breathlessly. "We can't do this. It's just not right."

His voice was wistful when he replied. "It sure felt right to me."

He was still lying half on top of her. Their legs were still tangled, his fingers still buried in her hair. She pressed her hands against his shoulders, pushing him upright. "I don't know why this keeps happening," she almost wailed as she struggled to sit up and scoot farther away from him. "We've been friends for more than a year. I don't do this sort of thing with my other male friends."

"I should damn well hope not," Shane growled, pushing a hand through his hair.

She gave him a fierce look. "It shouldn't happen with you, either."

"I think it's too late to keep things from changing now."

Kelly gave a despairing moan.

Shane twisted again on the couch, looking at her intensely. Too intensely, she thought, aware that her hair was still tousled, her lips still damp from his kisses, her cheeks still flushed from their passion. "Look, I know this isn't something either of us expected to happen— but it has," he said bluntly. "Why does it frighten you so much?"

"You never acted like this with me before."

"Like what?"

"You used to treat me like one of the family. Now..."

"Now I treat you like a woman I find extremely attractive."

She gulped. "That's..."

He lifted his hand to touch her trembling lower lip with the tip of one finger. "Now I kiss you the way a man kisses a woman he wants."

Her lungs convulsed. "Shane," she said with a gasp. "Don't…"

"There's something happening between us. I know you feel it, too. Why does it frighten you?"

"*Why?*" She stared at him, wondering if he could really be that dense. "You have to see what a huge mistake this is. What a disaster it could be."

"Why don't you explain it to me?"

She made a sound of frustration. "We're family! Maybe not by blood," she added when he started to speak, "but my connection with Brynn has brought me into the family and I don't want to lose that."

"Of course not. And there's no way your relationship with them will ever change. They're all very fond of you."

She leveled a chiding look at him. "Let's be realistic here. You're a member of the family. They've known you most of your life. I'm an old friend of your cousin, who has only been around for a little more than a year. If an unpleasant situation develops between us, I'm the one who'll have to stay away so the others won't be uncomfortable. You've seen what happened with Cameron and Amber, how awkward everyone acted around them the other night. How long do you think it will be before one or the other disappears from the group entirely? I don't want to end up in that position with your family."

"It's not going to happen that way."

"Does that mean *this* is never going to happen again?" She waved a hand to generally indicate everything that had gone on between them that evening. "We can go back now to the way it was between us before?"

Shane hesitated, then slowly shook his head. "I don't think that's going to happen, either."

Frowning, she looked at him warily. "What do you mean?"

"I can't go back," he answered simply. "I can't see you as a pal or a cousin anymore. Every time I look at you now, I find myself thinking about how beautiful you are. When I touch you, even by accident, I can't stop myself from wanting to touch you again. And I can't stop wanting to kiss you. Wanting more. I don't know when everything changed. Maybe I've felt this way from the beginning and I just couldn't pretend anymore. But I can't go back."

She gulped. "So what are you suggesting?"

"The way I see it, we have two options. We can stay away from each other—make an effort not to be alone together again, at least for the foreseeable future…or we can find out exactly where this leads."

Stay away from each other? The thought of not seeing Shane punched a hole in her heart. He had become so much a part of her life that his absence would leave an emptiness she wasn't sure she would ever be able to fill. That painful realization made her all the more aware of how very much was at stake with her reply. "How can we…find out where it leads?" she asked, using his words.

"I, er, don't know, exactly." He sounded uncharacteristically uncertain. "Maybe we could—you know—go on a date or something?"

"A date?" she repeated, twisting her fingers in her lap so tightly that her arms ached.

"Yeah. Maybe a movie. We've seen lots of movies together."

But they had never considered their outings "dates," she thought. Before, they had been two friends who simply enjoyed spending time together. Now, they would be going out as…what? Potential lovers? That possibility made her toes curl in her shoes. "I don't…"

"If you aren't interested, I'll understand," he assured her. "You won't have to worry about my bothering you. I won't kiss you again, either, if you ask me now to stop. Whatever happens, I don't ever want you to be afraid of me, Kelly."

She wasn't afraid of Shane. But she was utterly terrified of the way she felt when he kissed her. So what she *should* do was politely decline his offer and make an effort to hold him at a safe distance from now on, even if that meant never being alone with him again.

But what she said was, "I suppose we could go to a movie or something—on one condition."

"What condition?"

"No one else can know it's a date," she said firmly. "As far as anyone else will know, we'll just be a couple of friends hanging out together for an evening."

He frowned. "Isn't that what a date is?"

"You know the difference," she chided. "I don't want anyone to know anything has changed between us—not our friends or our family. That way, if we discover that this is all a big mistake—which I'm sure we will—we can put it all behind us without anyone else being the wiser."

"You mean you want to date secretly?"

She nodded. "At least for now."

He thought about it a moment, then nodded. "Okay."

"Okay?"

"Yeah. It's no one else's business, anyway, right?"

"Er…right."

"So, you want to call it a night, or should we head for your bedroom and find out where *that* leads?" he asked cheerfully.

Kelly choked and then glared at him when she realized he was teasing her. "That wasn't funny."

He grinned. "Okay, so we'll start with a movie." He pushed himself off the couch and headed for the door. "Tomorrow night at seven?"

She rose, wondering what on earth they were doing. "Fine."

"I'll look forward to it. But I won't tell anyone," he added, his blue eyes glinting now with his usual humor.

"Good." She gave him what she hoped was a quelling look.

Shane left without another word. Kelly promptly collapsed onto the couch and hid her face in her hands. At least she knew she wouldn't spend the night worrying about what to tell her father. She had more pressing problems to worry about.

A date with Shane? *What had she been thinking?*

Kelly felt like such a fool. Her bedroom looked like a tornado had swept through it, leaving piles of clothing in its wake. She must have donned and discarded half a dozen outfits, and she still wasn't happy with what she was wearing.

She couldn't believe she was acting this way over a simple movie date with Shane.

She was considering changing again when the phone rang. Maybe, she thought with a jolt of cowardly optimism, Shane had to cancel their plans for the evening. But the caller was Brynn. "Have you made a decision yet about your father?'' she asked, having heard about the situation when she and Kelly had talked earlier that day.

''No, not yet.'' She didn't add, of course, that she'd hardly given her long-absent father any thought. She'd been much more preoccupied by worrying about her date with Shane.

''Would you like to have dinner with Joe and me this evening? We can talk about it, if you like.''

Keeping her tone very casual, Kelly replied, ''Thanks, but Shane and I are going to a movie this evening.''

Brynn seemed to find nothing at all unusual about that. ''Oh, that's good. You need a night just to have fun, and you can always count on Shane for that.''

''That's what he claims,'' she said lightly.

''How did you do on your test today?''

''It was easier than I expected.'' Kelly was relieved that Brynn had changed the subject so easily. ''How was yours?''

''I did pretty well, I think.''

''One more semester behind us.''

''Ain't it great?'' Brynn agreed.

Kelly eyed her reflection in the full-length mirror across the room. Her latest outfit choice was a snug-fitting, blue-and-tan striped sweater with khaki cargo pants and brown boots. Too casual? Was the scooped neckline of the sweater too low? Maybe she should put the black pantsuit back on, the one she had eliminated earlier as too dressy for a movie date.

''Kelly?'' Brynn broke into her thoughts, sounding as if she had tried before to get her attention. ''Are you still there?''

''Sorry,'' she said with a wince. ''Static on my end.'' All between her own ears, of course.

"I'd better let you go. Shane will rib you if you aren't ready when he picks you up."

"Yeah. He'd be convinced I spent extra time on my appearance for him," Kelly joked lamely.

Brynn laughed. "You'd never hear the end of it. Have a good time, okay? You deserve a night out to relax."

Though she couldn't imagine this evening was going to be particularly relaxing, she said only, "Thanks. I'll talk to you tomorrow."

She groaned as she hung up the phone. What was she doing? She had just deliberately misled her best friend. What made her think she and Shane could get away with this?

Her only hope was that tonight's "date" would turn out to be a one-time experiment. She wanted to believe they would realize very quickly that what they felt for each other was nothing more than a deep, caring friendship and that the sexual overtones they'd battled recently were only a temporary aberration. By the time this evening ended, they could both quite likely be laughing at how foolish they had been to imagine a depth to their relationship that simply wasn't there.

And then her doorbell rang and her pulse rate went crazy and her palms went damp, and she wondered if she really had lost her mind.

She should have worn the pantsuit, she fretted as she made her way slowly toward the door. She'd dressed too casually. Would Shane interpret it to mean that she wasn't taking this date seriously?

"You look great," he said when she opened the door to him.

She was relieved to see that he had worn jeans, a denim jacket and a navy pullover with his usual Western boots. "Thank you."

Shane smiled ruefully. "I'm glad you didn't dress up. Would you believe I almost put on a tie? And then I realized how dopey that was since we're only going to a movie."

"How silly of you," Kelly murmured, glad she'd closed her bedroom door so Shane couldn't see the mess she'd left in there.

He made a face. "Yeah. Who'd have believed I spent ten minutes just trying to decide what to wear to see a movie? Dumb, huh?"

She cleared her throat, trying not to think about her own wasted hour and a half. "So what movie are we seeing?"

He named the latest big-screen blockbuster. "Have you seen it yet?"

"No, but I've heard it's good."

"It starts in forty-five minutes. If we leave now, we'll have time to stand in line for popcorn before the film starts."

A movie and popcorn. It sounded like a safe, pleasant evening, she thought. She and Shane had done this sort of thing dozens of times together, though usually with other friends along. There was no reason at all for her to be so nervous about it.

So why did her hands tremble when he helped her into her coat? And why did she have to take a deep breath for courage before she stepped outside with him?

She hoped they weren't making a serious mistake.

Chapter Nine

Shane had never considered eating popcorn a particularly erotic act. But sharing a container of popcorn with Kelly in the darkened movie theater was one of the most intriguing experiences he'd had in a while. Every time they reached into the container simultaneously, every time their fingers brushed, a spark of physical awareness seemed to leap between them. Did she feel it, too?

Every time their thighs brushed, his insides tightened in reaction. Did she know what she was doing to him?

He'd thought a movie would be a fairly innocuous way to spend this first, experimental date. Something they'd done so many times before that they wouldn't have to feel awkward about it. He hadn't really given enough thought to how cozy and intimate a darkened theater could be, even with other people sitting around them.

He tried to follow the film, but the action on screen

seemed bland and trivial compared to the much more interesting interplay between Kelly and him. Despite his efforts to concentrate on the plot, his mind wandered ahead to after the movie. What would they do then? Go out for coffee and pie? Maybe hit a club for espresso and jazz? Or he supposed they could go back to Kelly's place for cocoa and...

He shifted in his seat as his mind was flooded with possibilities of exactly what he and Kelly could do if they were alone in her apartment. Possibilities that had been occurring to him with unsettling regularity for the past few weeks. He brought that line of thought to a screeching halt. He'd had a hard enough time talking her into a movie. Anything more—at least on this first date—would definitely be pushing his luck.

"Is something wrong with your seat?" she asked in a whisper.

"No. Want some more popcorn?"

"Shh," someone hissed behind him.

Kelly giggled softly and reached into the popcorn container again. Her musical laughter made him smile—and then start fantasizing again.

They stopped for coffee and pie after the movie, Shane having decided that was the option least likely to get him into trouble. He noticed that Kelly seemed more relaxed now than she had earlier, and that pleased him. The dim lamp on the table between them glittered in her emerald eyes and brought out the gold in her hair. She was laughing as she recalled an amusing scene from the movie—a scene he didn't even remember—and he found himself transfixed by the flash of dimple at the corner of her mouth.

"You really are beautiful," he murmured. "Have I ever told you that before?"

Her smile promptly faded, to Shane's regret. He shouldn't have said that, he thought. He'd made her uncomfortable. But then he remembered that they were supposed to be on a date. That was the sort of thing she should expect to hear on a date.

"Umm...thanks," she said. "So what did you think about the way the movie ended?"

"I didn't pay a lot of attention to the movie," Shane answered, suddenly feeling reckless. "There was someone much more fascinating in the seat next to me."

Kelly's cheeks flamed, making her look all the more attractive, as far as he was concerned. "Stop saying things like that."

He rested his arms on the table and laced his fingers in front of him. "Why?"

"Well...because."

He grinned. "Very illuminating answer."

She gave him a sizzling look that only served to heat his blood a few degrees more. "You're embarrassing me."

"You don't like being told that you're beautiful? Has no one ever said it before?"

She rolled her eyes, as if wondering how she was supposed to answer that question. "It's just not the sort of thing *you* say to me."

"Not in the past," he agreed. "Things are different now."

She bit her lip, looking worried.

"I really do think you're beautiful," he said gently. "Does that displease you?"

"Well, no," she admitted, suddenly shy. "Of course not. I mean...it's nice that you think I'm...pretty—"

"Beautiful," he corrected her, enjoying her confusion.

"Anyway," she said quickly, her tone suddenly prim, "it's always nice to get a compliment."

"You're right," he agreed gravely. "So why don't you give *me* one?"

She frowned. "I beg your pardon?"

"Everyone likes to hear something nice when they're out on a date. Isn't there anything in particular you like about me? Some reason you agreed to go out with me?"

Her cheeks were as red now as the Christmas decorations around them. "You're asking me for a compliment?"

"I'll take one any way I can get it," he quipped, curious now about what she would say.

She shook her head. "Honestly, Shane."

"Yes, honestly, Kelly. What do you like best about me? My charm? My wit? My big blue eyes? My sexy smile?"

"Well, it certainly isn't your modesty," she muttered, making him laugh.

"Well?" he prompted.

"You do have a rather nice butt," she mused.

Caught off guard, Shane blinked. That was one answer he honestly hadn't expected. Now *he* was the one with warm cheeks. "That, er, wasn't exactly what I meant."

She looked quite satisfied at having disconcerted him. "Hey, you asked."

He frowned at her. "You agreed to go out with me because you like my butt?"

"It's as good a reason as any, I suppose," she mused, her smile almost feline.

"Anything else you want to mention?"

"Not at the moment." She scooped the last bite of

her apple pie into her mouth and pushed the empty plate away, looking rather smug.

Shane promptly fell a little harder for her. Kelly's wicked sense of humor was another attribute that had always appealed to him. She had often been able to "zing" him when he least expected it.

As far as he was concerned, the evening was going very well. He had no doubt that if this truly had been a first date, this was a woman he would want to ask out again.

He drove his pickup slowly back to her apartment, taking a winding route that allowed them to admire the elaborate Christmas displays along the way. "Have you finished your Christmas shopping yet?" he asked, to make conversation when she fell quiet as they got closer to her neighborhood.

"No, not yet. I was waiting until I finished my classes for the semester. I'll hit the malls next week."

"Are you going to put up a tree this year?"

She smiled and nodded. "I believe I will. I've never had a tree of my own before. Last year I was still using crutches and living with Brynn. Now that I have a place of my own, I'd like a tree."

"Real or artificial?"

"I'd like to buy a real tree. A small one. I love the smell," she confided.

"Be careful not to let it get dry. And make sure you don't leave the tree lights on when you aren't around to keep an eye on them. And don't…"

"Shane, I know how to take care of a Christmas tree."

"Sorry. Like you, I like the look and smell of a real tree, but I worry about the fire potential."

"I never realized you were the worrying kind," she teased.

"I just believe in being cautious," he answered repressively. "Christmas trees cause a lot of fires every year."

"Are you saying I shouldn't have a Christmas tree?"

Spotting a brightly lit Christmas tree lot ahead, Shane changed lanes and turned into the drive. "Let's pick one out."

He'd obviously caught her by surprise. "Now?"

"Why not? We're here. We're in the truck. You want a tree, right?"

"Right," she agreed cautiously.

He parked and turned off the engine. "So let's get a tree."

Her eyes lighting with interest, she reached for her door handle. "Okay. Why not?"

"I have never seen *anyone* take longer to pick out a tree."

"It's my very first Christmas tree. I wanted it to be right."

"What was wrong with the first couple of hundred you looked at?"

Unperturbed by Shane's teasing, Kelly stood back to admire the small spruce he had just carried in and set up for her. It really was a pretty little tree, she thought in satisfaction. Exactly what she had wanted.

When he moved to stand beside her and draped an arm around her shoulders, she smiled up at him, forgetting for the moment that things were different between them now. "Don't you agree that it's a nice tree?"

"It's beautiful," he assured her with a smile. "Are

you going to decorate it, or do you like it just the way it is?''

"Of course I'm going to decorate it. Just as soon as I buy some decorations.''

He tightened his arm a little, drawing her more closely against his side. "It really is a great tree, Kelly.''

"Thank you for helping me with it.''

"You're welcome.'' He brushed a kiss against her temple. "I enjoyed every minute of it.''

Her voice sounded a bit more breathless when she replied. "Even when I had to look at every tree on the lot?''

"Even then,'' he assured her. "While you were looking at trees, I was looking at *you*.''

She went very still when he cupped her face with his free hand. It was obvious that he intended to kiss her. This was the time when she had to decide whether she wanted this experiment to proceed, or to end right now, before it went any further.

She lifted her face to his, knowing he would read the invitation correctly.

Shane lowered his head and she went up on tiptoe to meet him. Her arms went around his neck, his around her waist. Their mouths met and fused. For the first time, Kelly cooperated fully with the kiss, holding nothing back. And her cooperation changed what might have been a merely spectacular kiss into an explosion of sensation that nearly knocked her off her feet.

She no longer tried to deny to herself that she found Shane more attractive than any man she'd ever known before. She didn't try to pretend any longer that she thought of him only as a pal, or a sort-of cousin. He was a handsome, sexy, compelling male and everything inside her responded to him—always had, though she had tried for so long to resist.

She couldn't resist any longer.

She closed her eyes, giving herself over to her other senses. The scent of evergreen tickled her nose, and she knew she would always associate that festive smell with this magical moment. Shane's body pressed against hers, and she could feel his warmth in her breasts, in her thighs—and deep inside her, where desire had begun to stir and simmer.

Shane drew a hand slowly down her back, tracing the shallow dip of her spine and then settling at her hip. He shifted her closer to him and she realized that she wasn't the only one who was becoming aroused by the embrace. That intimate contact with Shane almost shocked her into retreat again—but the anticipation building inside her kept her where she was.

Apparently emboldened by her participation, Shane changed the angle of the kiss and drew her closer. He made no effort now to conceal the extent of his reaction to her. Instinct made Kelly rock lightly against him. His reaction was a flatteringly heartfelt groan.

"Kelly," he muttered, cupping her face between his hands. "I feel like I've been waiting for this forever."

His mouth came down on hers again before she could answer. His tongue thrust between her lips. His leg pushed between hers, settling her even more firmly against him. This was no longer a tentative, first-date kiss. This was a passionate embrace that would forever change the comfortably platonic relationship they'd had before. Whatever happened from this point on, she realized dimly, she and Shane would never again see each other in quite the same way.

She was trembling when the kiss finally ended. And even more amazingly, Shane was, too.

He drew her to the couch and pulled her down into his arms. She made no effort to resist. When he lowered her to the cushions, she pulled him down with her, sliding her hands over his shoulders to lock behind his neck.

He nuzzled her temple, rubbed his lips across her cheek, kissed the tip of her nose and the faint cleft in her chin. He nibbled at her lower lip and traced her mouth with the tip of his tongue. Even as Kelly concentrated on the pleasure he gave her with his clever mouth, she was aware that his hand was also busy, slipping beneath the hem of her sweater. His fingers slid across her stomach, which contracted in reaction. He sketched a circle around her navel, then finger-walked up her ribs.

She moved restlessly beneath him, her breasts already tingling in anticipation of his touch. When he finally, gently closed his hand over her left breast, she inhaled sharply and involuntarily arched her back.

"You feel so good," he murmured against her mouth, his thumb circling her nipple through the lace of her bra. "All evening I've looked at you in this soft sweater and all I could think about was how soft you would feel beneath it."

She couldn't help laughing gently, ruefully as she thought of the piles of discarded outfits littering her bedroom. "I'm glad you like the sweater."

"I like what's *in* the sweater," he corrected her. "You could be wearing a grocery bag and I would think you're beautiful."

"You keep saying that," she whispered, reaching up shyly to push a lock of hair off his forehead.

"Only because it's true." He lowered his head and pressed a kiss against her throat, then moved his mouth even lower, into the deep scoop of her neckline. His mouth opened at the top of her breast, tasting the soft skin there. Beneath the sweater, his hand pushed gently upward, baring more of her to his thorough exploration.

Kelly had never thought of herself as beautiful. Did Shane really see her that way? She wanted to believe that he did. She gasped when his tongue swept beneath the lace of her bra to tease her distended nipple. Her hands clenched involuntarily, clutching his shirt. He lingered awhile—just long enough to drive her to the edge of insanity—and then he lifted his head. He kissed her lips again, very tenderly, then sighed and reluctantly withdrew his hand from her sweater. He slowly pushed himself upright. "I'd better not push my luck on our first date."

As she straightened her clothes and scooted up to sit beside him, Kelly bit her kiss-swollen lip, thinking that he wouldn't have had to push very hard at all.

He cleared his throat and shifted on the couch, making a visible effort to pull himself back together. "The Christmas charity dance is tomorrow night. I know Heather talked you into buying a ticket when she hit up the rest of us last month."

Trying to clear the fog of desire from her mind, she nodded. "It's a good cause. I didn't mind buying a ticket."

She knew Heather had persuaded Shane to buy two tickets to the dance. Kelly had wondered at the time— back when she was still trying to convince herself that it didn't particularly matter to her—who he would ask to accompany him. She had planned all along to go stag, since she hadn't dated anyone for a while and hadn't been looking for a relationship at this point in her life.

Had he already asked someone? Was she going to

have to watch him spend the evening with another woman now that she had discovered how very right it felt to be in his arms? That was one possible aspect of their secret relationship she hadn't considered before.

"Will you go with me?" he surprised her by asking.

She didn't know how to answer. She still wasn't ready to go public with the fact that they were dating. If something went wrong between them now, no one else would ever have to know about it. She wouldn't have to deal with pity or sympathy or awkwardness or even teasing.

"I'll meet you there," she suggested. "Since we were both planning to go, anyway, no one will find it odd if we spend time together while we're there."

Shane frowned. "You still want to pretend nothing has changed between us?"

"Yes. Please," she added when he acted as if he might argue. "I'm just not ready to let anyone else know, Shane."

Though he didn't look particularly pleased, he nodded. "If that's what you want. But there's no reason we shouldn't go together, is there? I've given you lifts to parties before."

"I...think it will be better if we go separately." She wasn't confident enough about her acting abilities to risk walking in at Shane's side and pretending there was nothing unusual between them.

"I'm surprised you're not suggesting we take other dates to *really* throw people off," he muttered.

She winced at his unwitting referral to her earlier thought. Even for the sake of their deception, she didn't like the thought of Shane having a date with another woman. "I don't think that will be necessary."

"Damn right," he growled, looking suddenly fierce.

"If you think I'm going to stand back and watch you spend the evening with some other guy..."

"Promise you'll treat me the way you always do," she said urgently, covering his hands with hers. "Promise no one will know...."

He scowled, but nodded. "If it's that important to you, I'll try."

"Thank you."

"I still don't understand *why* it's so important," he added in a mutter.

"I just want to keep this to ourselves for now," she said again. "I think I've explained my reasons."

He shoved a hand through his hair. She noted that his hand was steadier now, as was his breathing. But there was still a glint of hunger in his eyes, still a very faint flush of heat on his lean, tanned cheeks. He was holding himself under tighter control than his rather casual tone indicated, she realized in wonder.

He wanted her. Shane Walker wanted *her,* Kelly Morrison. She still found it hard to comprehend. How could he not understand why she was so reluctant to share this amazing development with anyone else?

"We never talked about your father tonight," he said as if the thought had suddenly occurred to him. "I still don't know what you've decided."

"That's because I haven't decided anything," she replied with a shrug. "I really don't know if I want to see him or not."

"Want to talk about it?"

"We've said all there is to say about it, I think. I just have to decide what I want to do." She smiled a bit sheepishly. "To be honest, I haven't given it as much thought as I should. I've, er, had someone else on my mind."

He liked that. He grinned, reminding her that his ego didn't need too many strokes. "Good," he said, reaching out to touch her lower lip with the tip of a finger. "Keep thinking about me."

"I didn't say you were the one I was thinking about."

Shane's smile only broadened. "I'd better go. Still have that hour-long drive ahead of me. Unless you want me to stay, of course."

She couldn't quite tell if he was serious. She hoped he couldn't tell how tempted she was to ask him to stay when she said, "You'd better go."

He sighed heavily, but rose, extending a hand to boost her to her feet beside him. She walked him to the door, where he kissed her lingeringly.

"I'd say our first date went very well, wouldn't you?" His tone was just a bit smug.

"It wasn't a catastrophe," she agreed, deciding his healthy ego had been inflated enough for one evening.

Shane laughed and kissed her quickly again before opening the door. "See you at the party tomorrow— pal," he added, his teasing tone indicating that he'd accepted her request to keep their new relationship secret. For now.

She was smiling when she closed the door behind him. The evening really had gone well, she thought cautiously, studying the small tree in one corner of her living room. If that had been a first date with anyone but Shane, she knew she would be practically dancing around her apartment, eager to call her friends and tell them all about the exciting new man in her life.

Unfortunately, she still found herself bracing for disaster, still worried that this whole, reckless "experiment," and the comfortable life she'd built for herself during the past year and a half, would inevitably come crashing down around her.

Balanced securely in a pair of strong male arms, Kelly reached out to carefully position a porcelain angel at the top of her tree. She took a moment to arrange the angel's long lace skirts and delicate feather wings. And then she said, "Okay, you can put me down now."

Dr. Joe D'Alessandro grinned up at her. "Oh, I don't know. I kind of like this."

She frowned sternly. "Behave yourself, Doc, or I'll tell your wife."

Brynn looked up from the candle-and-greenery arrangement she was creating on Kelly's coffee table. "No need. His wife is keeping a *very* close eye on him."

Chuckling, Joe lowered Kelly to her feet and spoke to Brynn. "Remember the day you moved into Tony and Michelle's guest house to be a nanny to their kids? I stopped by to make sure you'd settled in comfortably, and I found you sitting on Shane's shoulders, both of you laughing your heads off. I didn't like it at all."

At the mention of Shane's name, Kelly busied herself straightening ornaments on her tree. But her guests weren't paying attention to her as they reminisced. "I remember," Brynn said. "I was changing a lightbulb in a ceiling fixture and Shane gave me a boost. You asked why we didn't get a ladder."

"And Shane gave me such a smug look that I was tempted to punch him," Joe answered darkly.

"Shane always has been a flirt. And we didn't know at the time he was my cousin."

"No. At the time, I saw him as a potential rival." Joe suddenly looked cocky. "Not that he'd have been in the running for long. I had my eye on you then and nothing would have stood in my way."

"You can stop flexing your machismo," Brynn advised him dryly. "Even before I knew Shane was my cousin, I never thought of him as anything more than a very good friend."

Joe nodded in satisfaction, then turned to Kelly. "Speaking of Shane, is he going to that dance thing tonight?"

Kelly tried to look nonchalant. "I believe he said he'll be there."

Brynn frowned. "I wonder if he's bringing that redhead. Maya? Kayla?"

"Gayla," Kelly corrected, suppressing a shudder. "I don't think he's seeing her anymore."

"Are you sure you don't want us to pick you up?" Joe asked Kelly, sipping the mug of spiced cider she'd made for him earlier.

"Thanks, but I'd rather take my own car tonight."

"Is Amber going?" Brynn asked.

Turning away from the tree, Kelly shook her head. "When she heard that Cameron is bringing a date, she decided to stay away. She said she's not ready to see him with another woman yet."

"I suppose it was inevitable that he would start dating again," Brynn said with a sigh. "But it's a shame it had to be so soon—and right here at Christmas."

"He's probably thinking the sooner the better, for Amber's sake," Joe contributed. "The quicker she stops hoping he'll change his mind, the easier it will be for her to get on with her own life."

Kelly sighed quietly, noting that it was Amber who seemed to be suffering most from the breakup. And Amber who was staying away from her friends because it was too painful to continue to be with them now that she and Cameron were no longer together.

"Don't look so sad, Kelly," Joe said. "As much as it's hurting her now, your friend will get over this. Trust me, I've never seen anyone literally die of a broken heart."

"You're an orthopedic surgeon, not a cardiologist," she reminded him, forcing a smile.

"The point is that she *will* recover."

"Would you have recovered if you and Brynn broke up after you'd dated awhile?"

Joe grimaced. "Maybe," he said doubtfully, with an expressive look at his wife. "But it would have been the hardest thing I've ever done."

"That's probably the way Amber feels. She has loved Cameron for years."

"You're probably right." Joe glanced at his watch. "As much as we've enjoyed having lunch with you and helping you decorate your tree, we really have to be going. I have to stop by the hospital and Brynn will want plenty of time to primp and fuss for the dance."

Brynn punched his arm.

"I didn't say you *need* to primp and fuss," Joe reminded her. "I just said you would."

Joe and Brynn were still teasingly fussing when they left a short time later. Kelly saw them off with a smile and a wave, and then turned to study her newly festive living room. It looked nice, she decided. Like a real home at Christmastime.

Though it was only a small, few-frills apartment, this felt more like a home to her than anyplace she had lived since her mother fell ill. Everything had been going along so nicely—and then Shane and her father had both made unexpected overtures that threatened to change everything.

Just as she'd been unable to stop the change in her relationship with Shane, she knew she was going to be forced to make some sort of decision about her father. She couldn't ignore his request forever. She only wished it hadn't come at a time when she was already feeling overwhelmed by so many other pressures.

She spent the remainder of the afternoon straightening her apartment and doing some laundry. And then it was time to get dressed for the dance. She didn't have to debate this time about what to wear. This was the perfect occasion to wear the red dress she'd bought on the shopping trip with Brynn.

Yet the dress that had seemed so perfect when she'd tried it on in the store suddenly looked different when she donned it in her bedroom. The spaghetti straps left a lot of bare skin above the low bodice. The clingy fabric left little to the imagination about her figure. And the skirt was rather short, making her legs look longer than usual, an illusion reinforced by flirty red sandals—low-heeled, of course, since her limp made high heels too precarious.

Maybe she should change into the black satin pantsuit she'd worn for the holidays last year to cover the then-fresh scars of her operations. Those scars were still there, but they had faded considerably, and the shimmering hose she wore further camouflaged the ones on her legs, though the one on her arm was still revealed. She had never been particularly embarrassed by her scars. She knew exactly how fortunate she was to have come through that accident as well as she had. She considered her recovery a testament to Joe's surgical skills. A limp and a few scars were of little significance when she considered that she could have spent the rest of her life in a wheelchair.

It was that bracing thought that made her lift her chin and decide to wear the dress with confidence. Brynn had said it looked good; Kelly would trust her friend's judgment.

As she donned a swingy, black evening coat in preparation to leave, she couldn't help wondering what Shane would think about the dress.

Chapter Ten

Shane was beginning to get concerned. He'd been at the country club at which the charity dance was being held for nearly forty-five minutes and Kelly still hadn't arrived. He'd asked around, but no one had heard from her. Brynn and Joe had explained that they'd offered her a ride, but she'd wanted to bring her own car. They didn't know why she was late.

Where was she, damn it? He tugged irritably at the bow tie that felt as if it was choking him. He hated evening clothes.

"Hey, Shane. You look bored. Thinking of bolting already?" Michael Chang asked, approaching with a glass of wine in one hand.

He forced a smile. "No, I can tolerate it awhile longer. Where's your date?"

Michael grimaced wryly. "She and Heather went to

the ladies' room. Why *do* women want to do that in groups?''

''Why else? So they can talk about us. I like Judy, by the way.''

''Yeah, me, too. It's our third date. So far, so good.'' Michael took a sip of his wine, then asked, ''How come you didn't bring anyone tonight?''

Scanning the crowded, elaborately decorated ballroom, and still seeing no sign of Kelly, Shane replied, ''There wasn't anyone in particular I wanted to bring.''

It was a lie, of course, but he'd made that stupid promise to Kelly. He wished he knew what was keeping her. Maybe he should try calling her apartment.

He glanced across the room to where Cameron stood with his statuesque blond date, Julie Fields. They were talking with Scott Pearson and Scott's companion, Paula, the woman Heather disliked so intensely. Shane suspected that Paula figured prominently in the ladies' room gossip.

Heather was determined to keep her brother from becoming Paula's fourth husband. Not that Shane thought there was any danger of that. In his opinion, Scott and Paula were merely having a little fun until something better came along.

''Have you met the woman with Cameron yet?'' he asked Michael.

''Yeah. She's a weekend anchor on local TV—I forget which station. Cameron said she's got her eye on a network spot eventually, and he thinks she'll get there. He seems to admire her, but I don't think there's anything more to it.''

Shane shook his head. ''It will be a while before Cameron gets involved again. His usual pattern is to play the field after a breakup.''

"Too bad Amber didn't come tonight. She usually enjoys things like this."

"She wouldn't have enjoyed it tonight," Shane murmured, glancing again at Cameron, who had the anchorwoman draped all over him at the moment.

Following Shane's look, Michael grimaced. "No, probably not."

Michael's friend, Judy, joined them then. A sweet-faced, generously rounded young woman, she worked at the airport where Michael's air-charter service was based. She chatted with Shane for a moment, then persuaded Michael to dance with her, leaving Shane to worry again about where Kelly was.

It was probably a good thing he was alone when he finally spotted her. He suspected that if he'd been in the middle of a sentence, his voice would have trailed into stammering incoherence. As it was, he must have frozen for a full minute before he got himself under control.

She looked…stunning.

Reminding himself that Kelly wanted him to act normal—whatever that was—he headed across the room toward where she stood visiting with Joe and Brynn. As he made his way through the well-dressed crowd, he practiced suitably casual greetings in his head.

"Where have you been?" was what came out when he reached her.

He couldn't read anything in particular in her expression when she turned to reply. "Oh, hi, Shane. I was just telling Brynn and Joe that when I went out to my car this evening, it wouldn't start. It kept making a terrible, grinding sound. I finally just called a cab."

"See? You should have let us pick you up," Brynn fussed. "Why didn't you call when your car wouldn't start?"

"I figured you'd already left," Kelly explained with a slight shrug that drew Shane's attention again to the soft expanse of shoulder revealed by her frivolous little dress.

He cleared his throat. "When's the last time you had your car checked out? What if something like this had happened on a deserted road?"

"Don't fuss at her now, Shane. You sound like an annoying older brother," Brynn chided him. "You haven't even told her how pretty she looks tonight."

"Oh. Yeah, you look great," he said lamely, motioning awkwardly toward Kelly's dress.

Brynn rolled her eyes. "Try to control your flattery, you'll embarrass her. Trust me, Kelly, any guy here who isn't family is going to think you look drop-dead gorgeous."

Shane scowled. *He* thought Kelly looked drop-dead gorgeous. She just wouldn't allow him to say so. And he didn't like the thought of any other guy thinking of her that way. He and Kelly weren't family, damn it. If only he could convince her to let him remind others of that significant fact.

"Speaking of guys," Brynn continued with an arch smile, "there's someone here I want you to meet, Kelly. His name is Steve Carter and he's a single surgeon who just moved to Dallas. He doesn't know many people here yet. He works at the hospital with Joe and he's here tonight with the hospital administrator and his wife. Steve is probably eight or nine years older than you, but he's really nice. I think you'll like him."

"Brynn," Kelly interrupted, just as Shane was prepared to do so. "I'm really not in the mood for a fix-up right now. I just got here, for Pete's sake. Let me take at least a few minutes to have some refreshments and greet my friends.''

"I'll take you over to the gang," Shane volunteered. "Cameron will probably want to introduce you to his date."

She made a face. "Do I want to meet her?"

He shrugged. "From what I've heard, she's okay. A bit predatory, but she is a television reporter."

"I just can't help thinking about poor Amber."

Shane hoped she wasn't starting to compare their budding relationship with the disaster between Cameron and Amber again. "Come say hi to everyone," he said. "They've all been asking about you."

"Oh, look, Joe, there are the Lamberts. We should go speak to them," Brynn said, touching her husband's arm. "Kelly, we'll see you later. Let us know if you need a ride home."

"I have to pass her apartment on my way home," Shane said casually. "I'll drop her off."

Neither Brynn nor Joe seemed to find anything remarkable about his offer. And why should they? he asked himself. He was getting as paranoid as Kelly.

He placed a hand on her arm to guide her through the crush of people mingling at the charity dance. He didn't know that many people in attendance, outside his own cozy circle of friends, so they weren't interrupted as they made their way slowly across the room.

"Why didn't you call me when your car died?" he asked. "You know my cell phone number."

"I decided it would be quicker to just call a cab— even though it was a bit expensive," she added ruefully.

"I would have come after you. No one would have found it unusual if you called me for help."

"By the time you picked me up and drove back here,

the dance would have been half over. Stop fussing, Shane, I took care of it.''

"I was worried," he said simply.

"I didn't mean to worry you."

"I know." They were only ten feet away from their friends when he lowered his voice and said, "By the way, you look stunning. You're the most beautiful woman in the room."

He heard her choke just as the others noticed them.

"Kelly, there you are!" Heather hurried toward them. "I was beginning to think you weren't coming. You look great! Love the dress."

"Thank y—"

"Can you believe Scott brought *Paula* to this dance? I swear he only did it to annoy me, since she obviously hates this sort of thing. He…"

Still talking, Heather drew Kelly away from Shane's side. Mentally repeating his promise to her, he let her go, but he was unable to stop looking at her. It really *was* a great dress. But Kelly didn't need glamour and glitter to turn him on; he found her every bit as appealing in jeans and T-shirts.

"What held her up?" Scott asked, nodding after Kelly and his gossiping sister as he approached with the much-maligned Paula on his arm.

"Her car wouldn't start. Sounds like a dead battery— maybe the alternator." Shane almost growled the answer, still cold inside at the thought of Kelly being stranded on some dark, lonely road with a dead battery. Anything could have happened to her.

"What did you do, chew her out? You're still glaring at her."

He made a deliberate effort to smooth his expression.

"I pointed out that she should take better care of her car."

"I'll bet you did." Scott grinned. "Probably sounded a lot like some of the conversations I've had with Heather. She's doing better now, but she used to think the warning lights on her dashboard were merely hints that she should have her car serviced when she had some time to spare."

Again, Shane was struck by the way everyone seemed to think of him and Kelly as family—cousins, perhaps, or even a sibling-type relationship. No one seemed to suspect that what he felt for Kelly was anything *but* fraternal. How could they not see the truth in his eyes when he felt as if it burned there like a neon sign?

Maybe he and Kelly could keep this new development a secret, after all. Though he didn't know how long he could continue the pretense, he thought as he realized exactly how many pairs of appreciative male eyes were focused on Kelly at that very moment.

"Excuse me," Paula said, her hands on her hips, her generous breasts sticking out provocatively as she stood defensively. "I happen to take very good care of my car. I have the oil and filters changed and the tires checked every three thousand miles. When I was in college and didn't have money to pay someone to do it, I changed the oil myself."

Shane smiled to himself as he thought that money was certainly not an issue for Paula. Alimony and divorce settlements from three wealthy, older ex-husbands had given the thirty-something—she would never admit how far past thirty—divorcée the freedom to live on her own terms now. Scott gazed indulgently at her, obviously having no interest in whether or not she could change the oil in a car.

While Shane had experimented a bit with relationships based on nothing more than physical attraction, he had long since decided he needed more. The women he admired most—his stepmother, his aunts and cousins, Judge Carla D'Alessandro—were all woman of intelligence, competence and integrity. Women who were perfectly capable of taking care of themselves, but valued family above all else. Women who stood beside, not behind, their equally competent mates.

He found his eyes turning toward Kelly again. Kelly, who had been on her own for a long time. Kelly, who had pursued her advanced degree with unwavering determination, who had fought her way back from a terrible car accident, enduring two operations, nearly six weeks of hospitalization, months of painful therapy and occasional lingering discomfort from the resulting quarter-inch difference in the length of her legs. And she had come through it all with a positive attitude, and an optimism he had always admired.

Other people might have complained about the bad luck of being involved in that accident. Shane had heard Kelly say several times that she felt fortunate the accident hadn't been worse, that she had come through alive and still able to walk, and to have made so many friends as a result of the accident.

Kelly was a very special woman, he mused. He suspected the reason no other woman had particularly interested him during the past year and a half was that no other woman compared in his mind to Kelly. Why hadn't he done something about it earlier? Was it because he'd instinctively sensed her fears—or because he had been battling some of his own?

"C'mon, Scott, dance with me," Paula said, tugging

his hand. "If we have to spend an evening at a charity dance, we might as well enjoy the music."

Scott gave her a lazy nod. "Sure. See you later, Shane."

"I really dislike that woman," Heather muttered as she and Kelly rejoined Shane, Heather glaring seethingly after her twin and his date.

"Get a life, Heather," he replied with the affectionate bluntness of a very long friendship. "Stop worrying about Scott."

"What if he marries her? I do not want that woman to be the mother of my nieces and nephews."

"He's not going to marry her. He can't afford to marry her. She likes 'em old and rich, remember? She and Scott are just friends."

Heather sighed. "I hope you're right."

"Speaking of *your* social life, I thought you were bringing someone tonight."

The sigh that escaped her this time was even more heartfelt. "I was. I had a date with a homicide detective. His pager went off two minutes after he arrived at my place to pick me up. He said he'll probably be tied up for hours. I thought about just staying home, but after spending more than an hour getting ready for this thing, I wasn't about to let my efforts go to waste."

"Your efforts paid off," he assured her, looking away from Kelly long enough to notice that Heather did look exceptionally nice in a deep green dress embellished with sparkling gold threads, a theme repeated in the gold stuff woven into her upswept auburn hair. "Very festive."

She caught his arm. "Come dance with me. I want everyone to see how gorgeous I look."

Shane glanced at Kelly. "You two go ahead," she

said with a smile. "I'm going to talk to Michael and Judy. And I'll introduce myself to Cameron's friend."

"Save me a dance," he ordered.

She lifted an eyebrow. "You know I don't dance."

"You will tonight." With that, he turned and gave in to Heather's tugging at his arm.

"That was nice of you, Shane," Heather announced as she claimed a few inches of dance floor and turned in to his arms.

He told himself to concentrate on his dance partner and not the slender woman in the flame-red dress across the room. "What?"

"Offering to dance with Kelly. The only time I see her get self-conscious about her limp is when someone mentions dancing. I bet she danced very well before her accident."

Since Shane knew firsthand that Kelly still danced very well—but couldn't mention that without revealing too much—he merely said, "I just thought she might like to give it a try tonight."

Heather nodded. "Dancing with you will be comfortable for her because you're pretty much family and she knows you won't be making judgments about her, or anything like that."

Family. As much as he had always liked the word before, it was beginning to annoy him a bit when it was used so often in reference to him and Kelly.

Kelly had greeted all her friends, and Brynn and Joe had just introduced her to Dr. Steve Carter. They'd been making polite small talk for only a few minutes when Shane and Heather suddenly reappeared. "Kelly, did Michael tell you his big news? Oh, sorry," Shane said blandly, "Am I interrupting something?"

"Well, actually..." Brynn began.

Shane stuck out his hand to the tall, dark-haired man standing at Kelly's side. "I don't believe we've met. I'm Shane Walker."

"Steve Carter. Nice to meet you."

"I hear you're new in the area."

"Yes. I just moved here from Tulsa."

Without glancing at Kelly, Shane pulled Heather in front of him. "Let me introduce you to my friend Heather Pearson. Heather, this is Dr. Steve Carter."

"Doctor?" Heather's eyes lit with interest. "It's very nice to meet you, Dr. Carter."

"Please, call me Steve," he said with an attractive smile.

"I'd like to hear what you think of Dallas so far. Why don't you tell me about it while we dance?"

Heather, Kelly thought wryly, had never been bothered by shyness.

Steve Carter certainly didn't seem to mind Heather's directness. "I would be delighted."

Heather promptly towed him away.

Brynn made a sound of exasperation. "What just happened here? Shane, I was *trying* to introduce Steve to Kelly."

"Sorry," he said casually. "I didn't know Heather was going to abduct him."

Kelly, of course, didn't believe him for a moment. But apparently Brynn and Joe did, which was all that mattered to her.

"What did Michael tell you?" she asked Shane, remembering the excuse he had used to interrupt them.

"Oh. Right. He's buying into the air-charter service he works for. He's going to be a full partner in the business and they're planning to expand."

"That is good news. When did it happen?"

"The plans were finalized earlier this week. He said he hasn't mentioned it before because he didn't want to jinx it."

"Michael's superstitious," Kelly explained to Brynn and Joe.

Brynn lifted her eyebrows. "A superstitious pilot?"

Shane nodded. "You wouldn't believe all the rituals he goes through in the course of an ordinary day."

"Obsessive-compulsive?" Joe asked thoughtfully.

"Probably, but not so badly that it interferes with his job or mental health, so he doesn't see any need to change now. He just calls himself 'superstitious' and goes on." Shane turned then to Kelly. "Have you had an opportunity to dance yet?"

She shook her head. "No, but..."

"They're playing some slow songs now. Want to give it a try?"

"Why don't you, Kelly?" Brynn urged. "You used to love to dance."

"Oh, I don't..."

"It's great exercise," Joe agreed, smiling at her. "It'll be good for you, as long as you don't overexert yourself."

"There you go, Kelly. Your surgeon has ordered you to dance with me," Shane said cheerfully. "You have no excuse now."

She rolled her eyes. "Okay, I'm outvoted. But don't be surprised if I fall flat on my face."

"Don't worry. I'll catch you if you do," he assured her.

She gave him a wry look. "Why doesn't that reassure me?"

Laughing, Brynn gave her a teasing shove. "Go dance

with Shane. And if he gets rowdy, we'll tell Uncle Jared and he'll be grounded.''

Shane's laugh was a bit hollow, but Brynn didn't seem to notice. With a swallow, Kelly allowed Shane to take her arm and lead her through the crowd toward the dance floor.

Shane had just taken her into his arms when he muttered, "I really don't like this."

"Dancing?" she asked in surprise.

"No. Pretending."

"Shane, you promised."

"And I've been keeping my promise, haven't I? No one suspects a thing. But do you have any idea how hard it was for me to keep my mouth shut while Brynn practically threw you at that doctor?"

She focused on his bow tie. "She was just introducing us. He doesn't know many single people here yet."

Shane's hand tightened at her waist. "He can just make his own friends."

"Heather didn't waste any time. You didn't put her up to that, did you?"

"I didn't have to. She heard the words *single doctor* and went into action."

"Which you knew she would do."

"I hoped she would," he amended.

She looked up at him through her lashes. "If it makes you feel any better, I wasn't interested in him."

"Good."

He started to pull her closer. Kelly held back. "Dance like a cousin," she ordered.

Shane sighed deeply, but obligingly loosened his grip. Not that it mattered how circumspectly they danced, she mused. She still tingled all over just from being in his arms. She only hoped no one else could tell—including Shane, who needed no encouragement at the moment.

After another dance and another hour of conversation, Shane turned to Kelly as they stood talking to a few of their friends. "I've had about all the fun I can take. If you'd like a ride home, I can take you now."

"You're welcome to ride home with us if you'd like to stay a little longer, Kelly," Brynn offered.

She smiled and shook her head. "Actually, I am a little tired. I think I'll take Shane up on his offer. You're sure you don't mind, Shane?"

He shrugged. "I'm going practically right past your apartment. It's no trouble."

Joe chuckled. "You sound as if you're going to slow down in front of her building and tell her to jump."

Shane laughed. "Maybe I'll come to a complete stop, if she asks me nicely."

Kelly made a face at him, but said only, "I just have to get my coat and I'll be ready."

There was no question, of course, that Shane would accompany her inside when they arrived at her apartment. She didn't bother to ask and he didn't wait for an invitation. He simply followed her in, closing the door behind him. He waited until she turned on a lamp and the Christmas tree lights. And then he pulled her into his arms without giving her a chance to resist.

Not that she would have resisted, she thought as she lifted her face to his.

He held her so tightly, he almost squeezed the air out of her. And then he kissed her until her head buzzed from lack of oxygen. She didn't complain. Right now, she needed Shane more than she needed her next breath.

When he finally lifted his head, she sagged against

him, drawing in a long, unsteady breath. "Wow," she said after a moment.

"I've been wanting to do that all evening," he growled. "Do you know how tempted I was to kiss you on the dance floor?"

"Shane…"

"Don't frown at me like that. I didn't kiss you, did I? I did exactly what you wanted, behaved just like your older brother or favorite cousin. But I didn't like seeing you in this great dress and only being able to tell you that you looked 'nice.' And I hated having Brynn try to fix up you with some clown right in front of me."

Every word he said only added to her anxiety. She could only imagine how everyone would have acted if Shane had followed through on his impulses at the dance. If he had kissed her on the dance floor, acted possessive in front of the new doctor in town, their friends would have been stunned, and gossip would have flown. By tomorrow, the news would have made its way through two large families—the Walkers and the D'Alessandros. Everyone would be speculating about what was happening between Shane and Kelly. They would want to know how long this had been going on, where it was headed. How long it would last.

And then, if—*when*, most likely, she amended pessimistically—it ended, everyone would wonder what to say to her. Should they mention Shane to her, or would that be too painful? Should they invite her to intimate family gatherings at which Shane would be present, or would that be too awkward? It was exactly what was happening with Cameron and Amber now, she reflected sadly. Eventually, one of them would find the situation too uncomfortable and would simply drift away. It had already started to happen, really. Amber never would have missed a glittering holiday party before she and Cameron had tried dating.

Shane sighed. "Whatever you're thinking, I don't like it."

"I'm just not ready to be the subject of family gossip," she said apologetically. "There's too much else going on right now. School. The holidays. My father."

He nodded somberly. "I'll play along. For now. I don't want to complicate your life, Kelly. I only want to be an important part of it."

She lifted a hand to his cheek, tracing the firm line of his jaw with her fingertips. "You already are."

He kissed her again, this kiss so tender, so sweet, so filled with emotion that her chest ached. She could no longer deny to herself that she loved Shane—had probably been in love with him since he'd walked into her hospital room, introduced himself as a longtime acquaintance of her surgeon's and asked if she needed a friend in her new hometown.

"I can tell you now," Shane murmured, cupping her face in his hands, "that you were the most beautiful woman in the room tonight. I can tell you that I nearly fell flat on my face when I saw you standing under the chandeliers in your sexy red dress with those glittering stars in your hair and even brighter stars in your eyes. I can say that I wanted you so badly my hands started to shake—and that I want you every bit as badly now."

Once again, Shane had taken her breath away, this time with nothing more than his words. Her throat too tight to allow her to speak, she could only gaze up at him with her heart in her eyes. He wrapped his arms around her, lifting her high onto her toes as he kissed her again, this time with a passion that emptied her mind of everything but him.

"Are you going to send me away tonight?" he muttered between kisses.

She knew exactly how far her willpower extended— and it wasn't that far. "No," she whispered, trembling with terror and anticipation.

"More than anything else in the world, I want to stay. But I need to know this is what you want."

She wished he would just stop talking and take action. It was so much easier to simply follow his lead. But Shane demanded that she take an active—not a passive—role. He would not stay unless she asked him to. Did he know how hard it was for her to ask?

Of course he did.

He waited patiently. Implacably. His arms remained around her, his gaze held hers, but he made no other effort to persuade her. She found herself growing irritated with him. "Do you want to stay or not?"

"That wasn't the question," he reminded her gently. "I've already said I want to stay. What I need to know is whether you want me to."

"I said I wouldn't send you away."

He still wasn't satisfied. "Ask me to stay, Kelly."

It would serve him right, she thought, if she asked him to leave instead. But she didn't want him to go. She'd spent the entire evening pretending, disguising her feelings. She couldn't do so now. "Please stay," she said quietly.

The relief in his eyes told her just how badly he had needed to hear those words.

The stern intensity left his expression, to be replaced by a broad grin that was pure Shane. He swung her around, completely off her feet, lifting her high against his chest. She was forced to throw her arms around his neck for balance—and then she left them there because she wanted to.

"You're going to throw out your back," she warned him, her feet dangling over his arm, her red dress tangled around her thighs.

"No way," he assured her, nuzzling her neck. "You're as light as a feather."

"Big, strong cowboy," she teased, ruffling his uncharacteristically neat hair. "Even if you do look like a city boy in this tux."

"I could get out of this penguin suit in less than three minutes."

She swallowed, her fingers tightening reflexively on his shoulders as her mind filled with startling pictures. "Er...could you?"

"With the proper incentive, of course."

"And that would be?"

He nipped at her bare right shoulder, nudging her spaghetti straps out of the way. "You."

For a moment, her voice was frozen in her throat. When she had agreed to explore a deeper relationship with Shane, she hadn't been able to think beyond a first date. A few kisses. She'd known that kisses wouldn't be enough for long. But now that the moment of decision was actually here, her first impulse was to run. Her second was to stay and take what she wanted.

Making her choice, she pressed her lips to his.

Chapter Eleven

She must have taken Shane by surprise, because he froze for a moment, his mouth going still beneath hers. He recovered quickly, his arms tightening around her. And suddenly he was the one taking the initiative as his tongue plunged into her mouth to claim her. He was still kissing her when he carried her across the room and into her bedroom, where he lowered her to the bed and proved that he could, indeed, shed the tuxedo in less than three minutes.

He got rid of her simple little red dress in even less time. He smiled when he saw what she'd worn beneath it.

"For me?" he murmured, touching an almost-reverent fingertip to the frivolous red lace bustier.

Had she known when she'd dressed that Shane would be seeing the seductive undergarments? "Yes," she answered.

His smile deepened. "Thank you."

"You're welcome."

Why was she lying there smiling back at him? Why wasn't she more nervous? Why wasn't she trying to talk herself out of this? Why wasn't she reminding herself of all the possible repercussions, all the things that would probably go wrong?

Instead, she opened her arms to him. "Come here, cowboy."

He chuckled. "I love it when you talk dirty."

"Just shut up and kiss me."

He did much more than kiss her. He savored her. He mesmerized her. He transported her. He kissed her lips, her eyelids, her earlobes. He tasted her throat, her breasts, the soft skin below her navel. He touched the scars on her legs and then kissed them, too, to prove that they didn't bother him.

Kelly insisted on having her turn. She knew Shane so very well. Knew the way his coffee-brown hair fell over his forehead. The way his blue eyes crinkled when he smiled. The way his dimples appeared and then vanished with a capriciousness that had always fascinated her.

But now she learned even more about him. How his work-honed muscles felt as they rippled beneath her palms. The way his flat stomach contracted when she trailed her fingertips across it. She learned how it felt to rest her cheek against his chest, to have her nose tickled by the light dusting of hair there. She learned how to make him smile. How to make him gasp. And how to make him moan.

Lying on her back beneath him, she gazed up at him in wonder. He was the Shane she knew—but he was different somehow. His face was so achingly familiar to her, and yet he wore an expression that was so excitingly new.

She loved everything about him—everything she had come to know during the past year and a half, and everything she had discovered in the past half hour. She was deeply, desperately in love with Shane Walker, and while she wasn't yet ready to tell him, she was more than ready to show him.

She wrapped herself around him when he lowered himself to her.

Kelly learned then that she hadn't been the only one to predict this outcome to the evening. Shane was fully prepared to protect her from any unplanned consequences to their lovemaking. She appreciated his foresight, and the brisk, matter-of-fact way he took care of it.

She rose to welcome him when he joined them with one deep, smooth thrust. She gasped, quivered and then moved eagerly with him. The explosion came swiftly, rocking through her, curling her toes, forcing a cry from her throat. He held her, murmured her name, waited until she'd wrung every ripple of pleasure from the experience before giving in to his own need. He stiffened and gasped her name. Holding him closely, she thought how right her name sounded on his lips—and knew she would never forget this moment of pure joy.

No matter what happened next between them.

They didn't sleep. Kelly was too overwhelmed by their lovemaking, and Shane must have been, too. He couldn't seem to stop touching her, kissing her, looking at her.

"Are you tired of hearing me tell you how beautiful

you are?'' he murmured, stroking a hair away from her cheek.

She smiled. ''How could any woman get tired of hearing that?''

He kissed the end of her nose. ''You're beautiful.''

''Thank you,'' she replied with a primness that made him chuckle.

''I'm really glad I brought you home tonight.''

She gave him an exaggeratedly suspicious look. ''Are you sure you didn't sabotage my car battery?''

He laughed. ''I didn't. But if I'd thought of it...''

She pinched his ribs, making him squirm and laugh again.

When he was still, she rested her head on his bare shoulder and sighed lightly. He stroked her arm. ''Are you tired?''

''A little,'' she admitted. ''But not sleepy, really.''

''Me, either. I feel damned good, actually.''

She smiled, spreading her fingers over his chest. She could feel his heart beating beneath her hand. The steady thumping soothed her, and she drifted for a time, savoring the feeling of lying in his arms.

She broke the comfortable silence eventually. ''I've decided what to do about my father.''

''Have you?''

She nodded against him. ''I'm going to see him, I think. I'll call your uncle Monday and have him set up a meeting.''

''What made you decide?''

''Something you said,'' she admitted. ''About how you needed to see your mother again as an adult, just to satisfy your own curiosity.''

''Don't forget that my reunion with my mother wasn't a particularly happy one.''

"I know. And I'm not expecting much from this meeting with my father. But you were right, I think. I need to ask him why he abandoned me the way he did."

"You probably won't like his answer."

"I'm sure I won't. I can't imagine any justification for what he did. But I guess I need to ask."

Shane nodded. "Trust me, I understand completely."

"I knew you would. That's why I wanted to tell you what I decided."

"Are you going to have anyone with you when you meet with him? Or would you rather see him alone?"

"Alone, I think."

"Let me know if you change your mind."

"I will." She fell silent for a moment, then added, "I'm still really angry with him."

"Definitely," He agreed. "Saying it to him will help you put it behind you once and for all."

"Did you tell your mother how angry you were?"

"It wouldn't have done any good. She was too drunk to listen."

"So why haven't you talked to your father about how you felt about him during those unpleasant years?"

She knew when he stiffened that he didn't care for that particular question. "I've told you before that I'm not mad at my father for anything that happened in my childhood. I don't blame him for being in the navy, or because the court gave my mother custody instead of my dad when they divorced. He did the best he could."

Thinking of a twelve-year-old boy so deeply disconsolate that he'd chosen to risk running away and living on urban streets rather than to stay in his troubled mother's home, she still didn't quite believe Shane's denial. He had learned so young to mask his feelings, she mused, and there were still emotions he hid very deeply inside him. Was he hiding them even from himself? Was he ever haunted by memories of that unhappy phase of his life?

"What was it like, living on the streets of Memphis when you were only twelve?" she asked quietly, wondering if he would tell her or shrug the question away with an evasive answer.

She was beginning to think he wasn't going to answer at all when he shrugged and said, "It was pretty bad. I spent the entire two weeks scared and hungry and cold— praying that my dad would find me, hoping my mother would not."

"You were so sure Jared would find you?"

"I knew he would try. I left clues for him—things I knew my mother or the police would never understand, but my dad would. Of course, I didn't know my mother would wait nearly two weeks to call Dad and tell him I was missing. She either didn't notice for a while or she didn't want him to know how badly she'd screwed up."

"Why didn't you just call him yourself and tell him how unhappy you were?"

"I didn't know how to call his ship. When I tried to talk to him when he called, I made a mess of trying to tell him and he didn't really understand. He kept telling me he wished things were different, but that the court had given me to my mother and there was nothing he could do about it. I finally decided it was going to take drastic action on my part to make them change that ruling. No one really understood how unhappy I was until I ran away. After that, Dad wouldn't have sent me back to my mother even if he'd have had to go on the run himself, to keep me."

"And you never blamed him for not knowing how bad your home life was?"

"How could he have known? He was on a ship hundreds of miles away. He only had my mother's word that she was taking proper care of me. He probably thought I was exaggerating things a bit because I missed him and wanted him to come home."

Kelly bit her lip.

His tone a cross between exasperation and genuine curiosity, Shane asked, "Why do you seem to want me to be angry with my father?"

"That isn't what I want at all," she assured him quickly. "I'm just trying to understand you. Everything that went into making you the man you are."

Settling her bare body more snugly against his, he murmured, "I guess I can understand that, considering the circumstances."

"Do you still think about your childhood? About those two weeks you spent on the streets of Memphis?"

"I still have dreams about it sometimes," he answered after a moment. "Nightmares, sort of. I don't have them as often as I used to, and I think someday they'll stop altogether, but every once in a while I still wake in a cold sweat, with memories of those weeks in my head."

"Will you tell me about them?"

"I spent every penny I'd saved from allowance and birthday money on a bus ticket to Memphis, which is where my father had last been stationed. When I got there, I slept curled up in hidden corners. I ate what I could find. I talked a couple of store owners into paying me for sweeping their sidewalks, and I used the money they gave me to buy milk and overripe fruit. I washed up and changed clothes in public rest rooms, washing my spare clothes in the sink and laying them in the sun to dry. I lied to nearly every adult I talked to, but I never stole anything or got into trouble.''

"Did anyone ever try to...hurt you?" she asked, phrasing the question carefully.

"I didn't get close enough to anyone to give them a chance. I'd been living with a couple of quick-tempered drunks," he reminded her. "I'd learned to be careful—and fast on my feet."

"You must have been so happy to see your father."

"When I spotted him walking the streets looking for me, I was so happy and relieved that I couldn't even say anything at first. I just stood there with my mouth hanging open and my knees all weak and shaky. And then I started running, and I didn't stop until I was in my dad's arms.''

She lifted her head to study his face. "It's so obvious that you love your father very much."

"Of course." He sounded surprised that she would even need to point that out.

Propping her head on one hand, she used her other hand to trace his strong jaw with one finger. "After all you went through, how did you ever turn out so well?"

"I think my dad has a lot to do with that."

"Maybe," she agreed, "but I think it has as much to do with who you are. You could have turned out badly, could have been bitter and angry, but you chose to be better than that. I admire you very much, Shane."

He looked endearingly embarrassed. "Your childhood was no easier than mine. You've had a rough time since. But you've never given up on your goal of getting your education and you've done it with a positive attitude. I've never heard you complain. I admire you, too."

"Why would I complain?" she asked logically. "I've had some setbacks, but I've been more fortunate than a lot of people I know who were raised in foster care. Do you know how few foster kids are able to go to college? How many end up homeless after the system cuts them loose as soon as they turn eighteen?''

''I know the statistics,'' Shane replied. ''My father grew up in foster homes. He was so unhappy with the system that he worried constantly that I would end up there if anything happened to him. That was when he and I were on our own, after he found me in Memphis, before he knew he had family to turn to. When he first found out his siblings were looking for him, he wasn't sure it would be a good idea to be reunited with them after so many years. He changed his mind for my sake, mostly. He wanted me to have family if I ever needed them.''

''We've both been fortunate to have ended up where we are when so many things could have gone wrong.''

Shane suddenly smiled. ''As a matter of fact, I feel very fortunate to be exactly where I am. Here, tonight, with you.'' His slid his hand slowly down her bare side to her hip.

Kelly shivered in renewed pleasure. ''Speaking of where you are,'' she said, her voice suddenly husky, ''shouldn't you be going? What if someone notices that your truck is sitting in front of my apartment this late? We don't want to start the tongues wagging.''

His leg moved against hers. ''I don't care if the whole world knows I'm with you tonight,'' he said frankly.

The thought of anyone else finding out that she and Shane had become lovers was enough to send chills through her. She'd been unable to imagine how everyone would react if they'd suspected she and Shane were dating. But this...

Shane exhaled deeply. "You're going to insist again on secrecy, aren't you?"

"For now. Please," she added. "I'm still not ready to talk about this with the others, Shane. Let's just keep it between us for now, okay?"

"I'll try," he conceded grudgingly. "But it isn't going to be easy."

"Just for a little while longer."

"How long? When will you be ready to drop the pretense?"

"I..." How could she tell him, especially while they were lying together in her bed, that she still had doubts about whether this relationship would last? That she still worried something would go wrong and that she would be the one who paid the price for getting in too deep, too fast?

"How long, Kelly?"

"I don't know. Just...let me deal with my father first, okay?"

He hesitated only a moment before giving in. "All right. I won't push you. And I'll do my best to keep anyone else from finding out for now. But we'll have to tell them eventually. You know that, don't you?"

She bit her lip and kept quiet, thinking that Shane would agree this was the best choice if her prediction came true and they *did* decide this was all a mistake. He would realize then that she had saved them from a potentially awkward situation, and he would be grateful.

As for her...well, she didn't even want to think about how she would feel if Shane changed his mind about wanting her. She wanted to believe she would still be able to socialize with his family and their friends without letting a broken heart get in her way.

She shifted against the sheets as his wandering hand incited a new restlessness inside her. "Shane…"

His hand closed over one of her breasts. "Mmm?"

Her pulse rate accelerated. "You were going to leave?"

"Mmm-hmm. In a minute." He scooted farther down on the bed, replacing his hand with his mouth.

Kelly closed her eyes. "I suppose you can stay awhile longer," she murmured.

Shane didn't reply—at least not with words.

It was nearly three in the morning when he prepared to leave her apartment. She worried that he was too tired to safely make the hour-long drive, but he assured her he was wide-awake. No one would know what time he got home, he added. He'd deliberately built his house far enough away from his father's home to give himself privacy.

He kissed her lingeringly at the door. "Get some rest," he murmured. "I'll be back tomorrow to take care of your car."

"You're sure you don't have things to do at the ranch? I can always—"

"I'll be back," he repeated firmly. "Good night, sweetheart."

Sweetheart. Shane was always generous with endearments, she thought as she closed the door behind him, but there had been a new tenderness in his voice this time. If anyone had overheard him, they would have know something—everything—had changed. She could only hope he would try a little harder to disguise his feelings in front of the others.

She hadn't expected to sleep at all that night. She thought she would lie awake, replaying the events of the evening and worrying about the future. But she was asleep almost as soon as she turned out the light. She slept with the pillow Shane had used cradled in her arms, and the faint, lingering scent of his aftershave tickling her nose.

Her dreams that night were very pleasant ones.

Shane yawned as he and his father pored over a catalog of ranch merchandise, from which they were preparing to order supplies for spring calving. It was Sunday morning and the house was quiet, Cassie and Molly having gone to church. Jared had stayed home to catch up on some of the ranch business that had fallen behind during his vacation, and he'd called Shane to come consult with him.

"Think you can stay awake long enough to complete this order form?" Jared asked, sitting beside his son at the big desk in the ranch office.

Stifling another yawn, Shane rubbed his eyes. "Is there any coffee left in that pot?"

Jared reached for the carafe on the table beside him. "Just about a cup." He poured it into Shane's mug.

"Thanks." He sipped the warm, caffeine-charged beverage gratefully.

"You got in kind of late last night, didn't you? I was out checking on that sick calf at almost midnight, and I noticed you weren't home yet."

He shrugged, keeping his eyes focused on the catalog. "By the time the dance ended and I made the drive back, it was pretty late. I, er, took Kelly home after the dance. We talked awhile."

All of which was true, he rationalized, if not the full truth.

"Everything okay with Kelly?"

"Her car wouldn't start last night. She had to get a

cab to the dance. I promised her I'd look at it this afternoon."

"Any idea what the problem is?"

"It sounded like the battery or the alternator. I think I'll be able to fix it."

"Did she ever decide what to do about her father?"

There were few secrets in the Walker family. Shane knew Kelly was right about their changed circumstances making the rounds should word get out. "She's decided to meet with him."

"Has she?" Jared made a mark on the notepad in front of him. "What made her change her mind?"

"She wants closure, I think. Some answers, if she can get them."

Jared grunted. "I hope it goes well for her."

"You don't think it's a good idea?"

"You know how I feel about digging around in the past."

"I know how you feel. But you have to admit it paid off for you to be reunited with your siblings."

Jared shrugged. "I didn't have to deal with the bastard who fathered me. As for my brothers and sisters, we don't talk about the past. We concentrate on the friendships we've formed as adults."

"Kelly isn't expecting much from her meeting with her father. She's still pretty mad at him for running out on her and her mother."

"Can't blame her. He left his child alone to deal with the illness and death of her mother. What kind of jerk walks away from his own kid?"

"He, uh, he's in the military. He's been stationed overseas for most of his career."

"That wouldn't have kept him from picking up the phone. Or writing a letter. Or coming to get Kelly when her mother died. I was on a ship in the middle of the ocean when I found out you were in trouble, but I had little difficulty getting out to take care of you.''

Shane couldn't help thinking of the years he'd spent so miserably in his mother's home, waiting for a call from his father, praying for the visits that had come so rarely. His love for his father had never wavered during those years, but there had been times when he'd wondered why Jared didn't come home more often. He'd wondered why Jared didn't realize quite how bad things were in Shane's childhood home, even when Shane had tried to tell him. And—every once in a while—he'd been a bit angry with his father for not doing more to protect him from his mother's neglect.

He had never admitted that before. Not even to himself. Kelly had understood his childhood feelings even better than he had himself.

He looked up to find Jared studying him intently. ''Are you thinking about Kelly and her father now—or about us?''

Shane winced. His father had always been too damned perceptive. ''There might be a few similarities,'' he admitted. ''You were in the service. You were away a lot. Kelly's mother had terminal cancer, mine was a hopeless alcoholic. But you were there when I needed you most. You gave up your military career rather than let me go into foster care. And you've been a part of my life ever since. You would never have abandoned me the way Kelly's father did her.''

''There must have been times when you were mad as hell at me—and rightfully so. Your mother and I were young when you were born, and I knew zip about being a father. She and I were so miserable together that I started looking for excuses to stay away. I trusted her to take care of you, even if she didn't take very good care of herself. I was wrong.''

"You did the best you could.''

"I could have done better. I've always regretted that it took an act of desperation on your part to get through to me.''

Jared had never talked like this before about those early years. Shane didn't quite know what to say in response, except, "I don't blame you for my mother's problems or for a stupid court decision. I have never blamed you.''

"I know you don't. You've never blamed me for anything—not even when I deserved it. You've never given me any trouble and you've never resented that I've been a better father to Molly than I was to you at her age. You're a good son, Shane. I'm very proud of you.''

He swallowed hard, touched beyond words by his father's rare eloquence. "Thanks, Dad.''

"You know, of course, that I'm always here for you now. If there's anything you want to talk about, I'm ready to listen.''

Shane shifted in his chair, wondering if Jared was simply making a generalized offer or if he suspected that something momentous was going on in his son's life. There was nothing he would have liked better than to talk with his father about what had happened between him and Kelly. But he had made her a promise, and he couldn't renege on it now. "Er...no, there's nothing right now. But thank you.''

Jared nodded acceptance. "Consider it a standing offer. Now, about those newfangled ear tags.''

Shane tried to concentrate again on the order forms, but part of his attention remained on the conversation he'd just had with his father. Odd. That was the second time in recent weeks Jared had made obscure comments Shane hadn't known how to interpret. Was it only coincidence that the comments had come at a time when his relationship with Kelly was undergoing such a drastic change? Or did Jared know more than he'd admitted about Shane's feelings for Kelly?

There were times when Shane wondered if Jared knew him better than he knew himself. This was one of those times.

Chapter Twelve

"I'm really sorry I woke you, Kelly. I thought you'd be up by now."

Since it was a rare day, indeed, when Kelly slept until noon, she wasn't surprised that Amber hadn't expected her to still be in bed. She yawned delicately, then held the telephone receiver close to her mouth again. "Don't worry about it. I was just catching up on some of the sleep I lost during finals."

"I'm really sorry I disturbed you."

"Please, stop apologizing. It's past time for me to get up anyway." Turning her eyes away from the rumpled bed where her life had changed so dramatically only a few hours earlier, she tried to pay attention to the conversation with her friend. "What's up?"

"I was just wondering how the party went last night."

Amber's unusually subdued tone made Kelly frown in sympathy. She answered carefully. "It was the usual charity dance. Kind of dull. Not a lot of mingling between groups of acquaintances.''

"Did you see Cameron?''

"Yes.''

"Did you…did you meet his date?''

"Yes. She seemed pleasant enough, if a bit too polished—but that's probably because of her TV job.''

"I've seen her on the air. She's beautiful, isn't she?''

"She's attractive,'' Kelly admitted. "But then, she has to be, in her line of work.''

"Were she and Cameron…? Did he…?''

"They seemed to like each other well enough, but that was all,'' she replied honestly, though she hoped she wasn't raising Amber's hopes again.

"Did they dance?''

"Amber, don't do this. You'll only make yourself miserable.''

"I'm already miserable,'' Amber replied with a sniffle.

"This isn't helping. You can't sit around obsessing about what Cameron's doing or whom he's seeing. You have to find something else to do to occupy your mind until you get past this.''

"I just really miss him, Kelly.''

"I know you do,'' she answered softly. "I know you're in pain. And I wish I could help.''

"Just don't stop being my friend, okay?''

"Of course not. In fact, why don't we do something together this evening? We can go out for dinner—someplace really nice.''

"Thanks, but my mother's making dinner for me tonight. She's trying to cheer me up.''

Since Amber's mother had made no secret of her disapproval of Amber's affair with Cameron, Kelly hoped she wasn't overdoing the I-told-you-so's. "Some other time, then?"

"Yes. I'd like that."

"Great. Call me when you're free and we'll set up a time."

"Okay. Sure. Um...do you think I should call Cameron? You know—just to say hi?"

"No," Kelly answered honestly again. "It's over, Amber. You're just going to have to accept it."

With a deep sigh, Amber replied, "I know. It was just a thought. You're right, of course. I won't call him."

Relieved, Kelly almost sighed herself. Instead she said bracingly, "Call me when you want to get together."

"I will. Bye, Kelly."

Kelly hung up her phone, then groaned and rubbed her hands over her face. What a way to wake up after last night, she thought ruefully. Was fate sending her a reminder of what could happen to her if she wasn't very careful with Shane?

As if she'd needed reminding.

Because it had turned considerably colder during the night, she dressed in a bulky, waist-length sweater and loose-fitting carpenter jeans with warm socks and lace-up boots. She couldn't help smiling as she hung up the flimsy wisp of a dress she'd worn the night before. She'd enjoyed dressing up for the evening, but she felt much more herself now in her ultracasual clothes.

Shane had promised to come look at her car today, so she went to the trouble to put on a little makeup—a touch of eyeshadow, a quick sweep of blush and mascara. That was the extent of her primping for him. He had seen her dressed up and he had seen her in a hospital bed; much more than appearances were involved between her and Shane.

She'd just finished a late lunch of tuna salad and wheat crackers when her doorbell rang. Setting her plate in the dishwasher, she dried her hands and hurried toward the door, excitement zipping through her as she wondered how Shane would greet her today.

Her smile faltered when she saw that he was not alone. "Oh. Hello, Cameron. This is a surprise. Come in, both of you."

Cameron tipped an imaginary cap. "Auto club, ma'am. We got a call about an ailing car?"

Shane chuckled. "Cameron showed up at my place just as I was about to leave. When he heard what was up, he insisted on following me over to help."

She eyed Cameron doubtfully. "Do you know anything about fixing cars, Cameron?"

"I can hold a flashlight," the mechanically challenged reporter answered cheerfully.

"That's what I thought," she replied with a smile. "Pretty, but useless."

Not in the least offended by the teasing insult, Cameron laughed and reached out to drape an arm around her shoulders. "That pretty well sums me up."

Kelly felt a bit torn in her feelings about Cameron. She'd always liked him and enjoyed his dry humor, and she knew he was Shane's best friend. But she was very fond of Amber, too, and she couldn't forget the misery she'd heard in Amber's voice earlier. What a sticky mess this had become, she thought, biting her lip.

"Hand me your keys, Kelly, and I'll see what's wrong with your car." There was little expression in Shane's face as he studied her standing in the circle of Cameron's arm.

"Shane's not exactly Mr. Personality today," Cameron confided. "I don't think he got enough sleep last night. The cows must have mooed beneath his bedroom window or something."

Kelly stepped away from Cameron to search for her keys. Her eyes met Shane's briefly when she tossed them to him. For only a moment, she saw a glimmer of sensual awareness in his expression, and she felt an answering quiver deep inside her. But they must have hidden their feelings well. As sharply perceptive as he was, Cameron seemed to notice nothing unusual.

"You'd better grab a jacket," Shane advised when she started to follow them out. "It's gotten cold. Feels like winter out there all of a sudden."

Both Shane and Cameron were wearing jackets—Shane's lined denim, Cameron's battered leather. "I'll get my jacket and meet you at my car," Kelly said, turning toward her bedroom.

It *was* cold, she noticed when she stepped outside. A brisk wind tossed her hair and blew dried brown leaves across the parking lot. The wintry feel in the air reminded her again that Christmas was only two weeks away. She didn't have much shopping to do, but she needed to get to it soon. She'd drawn Brittany Sample's name, so she needed to buy something for her. She and Brynn always exchanged personal gifts, regardless of the Walker family drawing they both participated in now. She would buy small gifts for Heather and Amber, and for a couple of friends from her work.

Now she wondered where she and Shane would stand by Christmas. Would they still be secret lovers? Would their affair have become public knowledge by then? Or would it be over?

"Hey, zombie-face." Cameron waved a hand in front of her eyes. "Wake up."

She wrinkled her nose at him. "I'm awake. I was just thinking about Christmas."

He groaned. "That's enough to make *me* go zombie. I'll just be glad when it's over. The hype and syrupy sweetness is almost more than I can take. And of course I'm a villain now because I ruined Amber's holidays."

She winced. "No one thinks of you as a villain, Cameron."

He didn't look convinced. "Have you heard from Amber?"

"She called me this morning."

"How is she?"

Noting that his concern seemed sincere, she answered quietly, "She's unhappy right now, but she'll be okay."

Cameron pushed his hands into the pockets of his leather jacket. His usual insouciance was missing when he said, "I really didn't want to hurt her."

There was a part of her that still wanted to be angry with Cameron for hurting Amber. But she couldn't. She liked Cameron, and she knew how determinedly Amber had pursued him. Once he'd realized what a mistake they had made, he had done his best to rectify it before it had become even more painful. That Amber had been hurt was as much her own fault as Cameron's—if not more.

Amber had made the mistake of wanting too much, of ignoring reality to concentrate on her fantasies, Kelly thought with a somber look at Shane.

As if he'd felt her eyes on him, he looked up from beneath the hood of her car. "Looks like you need a new alternator. I'll run to the auto parts store and pick one up. It'll only take me an hour to install it—or two, if Cam helps."

Cameron chuckled.

"I really appreciate this," Kelly said to Shane.

"It's no trouble. I'll just get my tools out of the truck and take this one out first. You going to the auto parts store with me, Cam?"

"Sure. It's been a while since I've been to an auto parts store. Maybe I'll buy one of those pine-scented things to hang from the rearview mirror of my Corvette."

Shane pointed a finger at his friend. "You can go with me, but I forbid you to embarrass me."

Cameron grinned. "Have I ever done that?"

Shane only groaned and rolled his eyes.

"While the two of you are working on my car, why don't I make dinner for us?" Kelly suggested.

Cameron tilted his head like a puppy who'd just heard an intriguing sound. "Dinner?"

She smiled. "Lasagna? Spaghetti? Or maybe chili, since it's such a cool day."

"Chili sounds good," Shane said from beneath the hood of her car. "I haven't had chili in a while."

Cameron nodded. "I'll vote for chili."

Mentally running through the ingredients, and confident she had them all, she nodded. "I'll go get started, then. Unless there's something I can do to help you out here?"

Shane looked at Cameron, who was playing with the flashlight. "I think I have all the help I need out here, thanks," he said dryly.

As Kelly returned to her apartment, she couldn't help wondering if she'd just made a mistake. Would she and Shane be able to deceive Cameron during a cozy dinner for three?

* * *

Cameron didn't seem to notice anything unusual during a hearty dinner of salad, chili and jalapeño corn bread. Though conversation was brisk, they avoided any sensitive topics, talking about work and current events and music and films, but not about matters of the heart.

They were having pineapple sherbet for dessert when the telephone rang. Kelly answered it, then winced when she heard Amber's voice on the other end.

"I forgot to tell you something earlier," Amber said. "There's a sale at McGinty's Antiques next week. That little boudoir chair you like? It's going to be forty percent off."

"Really? Thank you for telling me. I might just buy it for myself for Christmas."

"I thought you'd want to know. I'd stopped in there yesterday to pick up something for Mom, and the manager told me about the sale."

"Maybe you and I can go together next week."

"Sounds good. The sale starts Wednesday. Want to go then?"

Before Kelly could answer, Cameron called out from the other room. "Hey, Kelly. Do you mind if I make a pot of coffee?"

"Go ahead. You know where everything is," she called back, then spoke into the phone again. "I'm free Wednesday, Amber. Let's plan to go then."

There was a long silence on the other end of the line. And then Amber asked, "Was that Cameron?"

She hadn't thought Amber had been able to hear Cameron's question through the phone line. She should have known her friend's hearing was hypersensitive when it came to Cameron. "Um...yes, Cameron's here."

"You mean you and Cameron are...?"

"Don't be ridiculous. Cameron and Shane are having

dinner with me. Shane worked on my car today and Cameron tagged along to help. I'm feeding them chili to thank them."

"I'm sorry. I guess I *did* leap to a ridiculous suspicion. I know you and Cameron are no more involved than...than you and Shane. I guess I'm still a little crazy from the breakup."

"I guess so," Kelly agreed weakly.

"I'll let you get back to your guests." There was a new note of wistfulness in Amber's voice now. "See you Wednesday, okay?"

"I'll look forward to it."

What a sad situation, Kelly thought as she hung up the telephone. All of Cameron's and Amber's friends were being placed in the middle between them, torn by divided loyalties. She found herself actually feeling guilty for having Cameron to dinner, which was ridiculous, of course.

Cameron pressed a cup of coffee into her hands when she rejoined him and Shane. "Your Christmas tree looks good," he commented, nodding toward that corner. "I like the minimalist look in decorations."

She made a face at him. "I'll admit I don't have many ornaments yet. This is my first tree. I'll have to build up a collection over the years."

"Are you the kind who's going to start a lot of sappy Christmas traditions?"

"I hope so. I love Christmas traditions. My mother used to tell me about her childhood Christmases in Germany. I've always thought if I ever have children of my own, I'd like to incorporate bits of my mother's Christmases into our family traditions."

The mention of having children made her suddenly aware that Shane was nearby, watching her. Though he had participated in the conversation at dinner, he had been a bit more subdued than usual. She found herself babbling to fill the gap. "What about you, Cameron? Does your family have any special traditions?"

Cameron's expression was suddenly hard. "Yeah. My mother goes on winter tours of Europe and my father spends a little more time than usual with his girlfriend. Of course they always made sure I had lots of presents under the tree Christmas morning. They were just never there to watch me open them."

Kelly looked at him in distress. "I..."

"Forget it," Cameron said abruptly, looking a bit chagrined that he'd revealed so much. "I tend to snarl during the holidays. I'll be glad when they're over."

He glanced at his watch. "I need to run by the newspaper for a few minutes. I guess I'll be going. Thanks for dinner, Kelly. I really enjoyed it."

"Thank you for helping Shane fix my car."

Shane snorted. "Yeah. He held the flashlight very well."

"I'm still grateful," Kelly said firmly.

Cameron surprised Kelly with a kiss on her cheek. "So am I. Good night."

With a sketched salute to Shane, he let himself out, leaving Shane and Kelly alone.

"What did he mean?" Kelly asked, turning to Shane. "That he was grateful for dinner?"

"For that—and because you're still his friend, even after what happened between him and Amber. He was a little worried that the gang would blame him."

"I wanted to blame him at first," she admitted. "But it didn't take me long to realize how unfair that was. Cameron and Amber simply made a mistake."

"Did they?" Shane toyed absently with one of the glass baubles on her Christmas tree.

"How can you even ask that? *Everyone* can see what a painful mess it turned out to be."

"I'll agree it ended badly, and was probably destined to do so. But was it really a mistake to try? Amber had fancied herself in love with Cameron for years. Until she found out for certain that it wouldn't work, how could she get on with her life, maybe give someone else a chance? And I think Cameron secretly hopes he'll find someone someday who'll really understand him—who can fill the emptiness inside him left over from his un-happy childhood. It might have been Amber—how would he have known for sure if he didn't give it a try? They'll both get over this, and they'll always know they gave it their best shot."

She stared at him. "I never realized you were such an astute observer of human relationships."

Shane's cheeks darkened a bit. "It was just a thought. Everyone keeps saying they made a mistake, but I think they just answered a question. Unfortunately, the answer was painful for both of them."

"And for their friends," she murmured.

"Few relationships take place in a vacuum. There are always others involved—friends, family. Children, in the case of most divorces."

Kelly swallowed painfully. Shane had just succinctly summed up her fears about *their* relationship.

He crossed the room to stand in front of her, his ex-pression suddenly sympathetic. "Still predicting disas-ter?"

"I..." Her voice trailed off as she bit her lip, uncer-tain how to answer.

He rested his hands on her shoulders. "We aren't Cam

and Amber. There's no reason to think we'll turn out as badly.''

Still biting her lip, she tried to find comfort in his words. But fear still lurked inside her, waiting to tarnish her time with him.

Shane kissed her lightly, teasing her lip from her grasp, rubbing his mouth against hers until she couldn't resist responding. She slid her hands up his arms, lacing them behind his neck.

He was right, of course. They weren't Cameron and Amber. But in some ways, the stakes were even higher for them, since their lives were intertwined even more intricately. Amber had a close family to turn to, as well as several good friends outside their "gang." Cameron had family, though they weren't close, and a large, loosely constructed network of friends he'd made through his work as a reporter. Cameron and Amber had complete, potentially satisfying lives away from each other.

For Kelly it was different. Every close relationship she had now was in some way connected to Shane. Her best friend—the sister of her heart—was his cousin. The other close friends Kelly had made during the past couple of years—Heather and Amber—had originally been friends of Shane. She had made a few friends at school and at work, but none who were as close to her as the people she knew through Shane.

Losing Shane at this point would be devastating. Losing *everyone*—being alone again—was an outcome she couldn't even bear to consider.

She pulled away from the kiss, stumbling a little, but quickly regaining her balance. ''Do you want another cup of coffee or something before you go?''

Shane frowned. "I didn't actually intend to leave just yet."

"You didn't get much sleep last night. And you've spent a lot of time away from the ranch on my behalf. I don't want to interfere with your work."

His frown turned to a scowl. "I'm perfectly capable of handling my responsibilities at the ranch. If you want me to leave, just say so. Don't make it sound like you're doing me a favor."

She was a little hurt by his sharp tone. Instinctively she took a step back from him. "I didn't mean..."

Shane reached out to catch her hand. "I'm sorry. I didn't mean to snap at you. I'm just...well, it isn't easy for me to keep pretending. It's hard enough for me to deceive my family...my dad. My friends. I didn't even like seeing Cam with his arm around you today, knowing he had no idea you and I are more than pals."

Her teeth gripped her lip again. Shane was starting to sound both impatient and possessive. How could they possibly keep this affair quiet if he acted that way? And yet she still panicked every time she thought about telling his family. "I asked for time," she repeated. "There's just too much going on for me to deal with right now. My father...Christmas... Maybe we could just sort of postpone this until after the holidays."

"'Postpone this?'" Shane repeated, his eyes narrowing, his voice going ominously quiet. "I'm not a dental appointment that you can simply reschedule for your convenience."

She was making a mess of this. Everything she said seemed to make it worse. "I wasn't trying to insult you. I just—"

"You still aren't willing to take a risk on me," he cut in flatly. "You're convinced that everything's going to go wrong between us and that you're going to be thrown out of the family or something equally ridiculous. Why can't you trust me that it won't happen that way?''

She shook her head stubbornly. Shane was making her fears sound groundless. Foolish, even. She thought *he* was the one being unreasonable by not acknowledging the very real basis for her concerns. Had he learned nothing from Cameron and Amber? ''You can't know that. It's still too soon to know what will happen between us.''

''Especially when you keep pulling away without giving us a real chance to find out,'' he retorted.

She crossed her arms over her chest and looked away from him. ''It's just so complicated.''

''Because you're making it that way. We're in some weird limbo—we aren't exactly family, but we can't tell anyone we're lovers. I feel like I'm having an illicit affair, which is crazy, because there's no reason we shouldn't see each other openly.''

Kelly thought again of the pain in Amber's voice. The regrets in Cameron's eyes. The discomfort in their friends' faces when they'd tried to socialize with both of them. ''I have my reasons.''

''And I'm supposed to simply go along with them?''

She lifted her chin. ''Not if you don't want to. We could go back to the way it was before. Forget any of this ever happened. No one will ever know there was anything between us. Nothing has to change.''

Shane was staring at her now in open disbelief. ''Kelly, everything has *already* changed. I'm never going to see you as a cousin again. I can't go back to kissing your cheek and pretending I don't want a hell of a lot more.''

She blinked back a film of tears, mourning the loss of

that easy, very special friendship. Afraid to risk losing even more.

Shane reached suddenly for his jacket. "I'd better go, before this 'discussion' turns into a quarrel."

She watched a muscle jump in his jaw. "You're angry with me, aren't you?"

"I just think it would be better if I leave now."

"I don't blame you for being annoyed. I realize my fears sound unreasonable to you. If we could just talk about it a little longer, I think you'll understand why…"

"I think we've talked enough tonight. I really need to go now."

"Why is it so hard for you to admit when you're angry? Wouldn't it be better if we talk about this?"

She didn't want him to leave mad. The holiday gatherings were rapidly approaching, and she and Shane would be expected to behave the way they always did. How could they pull that off if they weren't even speaking?

"Why don't we just 'postpone' that talk?" Shane shoved an arm into his jacket.

"Shane, you're obviously mad at me. Why won't you admit it? Stay and talk about it?"

"I'm not mad," he said from between gritted teeth.

She was both baffled and exasperated by his behavior. "You have a real problem acknowledging anger, don't you? Someone once asked me if I'd ever seen you lose your temper, and I said no. Maybe we should…"

"I do *not* want to talk about it." Shane had his coat on now. The look he gave her glittered with the temper he seemed unwilling—or unable—to express. "Why don't I call you tomorrow, after you cool down?"

"After *I* cool down? Shane, you…"

"Good night, Kelly. Thanks for the chili."

She stared at the door that he had closed behind him. "What was *that?*" she asked the empty room.

Shane had obviously been angry. Was it only because he was tired of hiding their relationship, or had she done something else to annoy him? How was she supposed to know why he was mad when he wouldn't even admit that he was?

She plopped heavily onto her couch, her shoulders sagging. What more proof did Shane need that they were making a mistake? They'd hardly gotten started with this…affair, for lack of a better word…and already they'd had a quarrel. Sort of. He'd already slammed out of her apartment. In a manner of speaking. He was furious with her. At least she thought he was.

Thank goodness no one else knew about this, she thought. Then mused wistfully that it might have been nice to be able to talk to someone right now.

Chapter Thirteen

"Shane, what in blazes is wrong with you today? That's twice you've damned near hit me in the face with your hammer."

Sitting back on his heels on the roof of the barn Monday morning, Shane winced. "Sorry, Dad. I guess my mind's wandering."

"I'll admit reroofing the barn isn't the most mentally stimulating activity, but it's got to be done before the worst part of winter sets in. You're the one who said today would be good for you."

"Yeah, it's as good a day as any. I'll try to pay closer attention to what I'm doing."

"I'd appreciate it. I'd like to have all my teeth for Christmas dinner."

Shane reached for another shingle. "We should be able to finish this today at this rate."

"Anything you want to talk about?" Jared asked casually.

There was nothing he would have liked better than to tell his father everything. To talk about how damned frustrating it was for Kelly to keep denying their involvement in front of everyone else. And for her to suggest that they "postpone" their affair until after the holidays... What was *that* supposed to mean?

Maybe Jared, having had more experience with women than Shane, could shed some light on Kelly's strange behavior, but since he was sworn to secrecy, he couldn't ask for his father's advice. At least, not specifically, he amended, carefully overlapping two shingles.

"I'm, um, having trouble with a woman," he admitted tentatively.

"Anyone I know?"

Shane would evade, but he wouldn't lie. "You know her. But I'd rather not mention her name right now."

"Okay. So what's the problem? Or would you rather not mention that, either?"

"She and I have been getting, er, close, but I can't get her to admit it. She won't even let me tell anyone we're seeing each other. She's so convinced that something will go wrong, she's all but written us off before we've even gotten started."

"What is she afraid of?" Jared asked without pausing in his work.

Appreciating the casual way his father was conducting the conversation, Shane kept his eyes focused on his own work as he chose his words. "Being hurt, I suppose. She's been let down before by people she cared about."

Like the father who had abandoned her. The grandparents who hadn't wanted to know her. The mother who had died. Had there been others who had failed to live up to Kelly's expectations, leaving her so wary of emotional attachments?

"And does she have reason to fear being hurt? Are your feelings for her the kind that will last?"

"I..." He cleared his throat. "She hasn't given us a chance to find out yet."

He could have answered more completely. He could have admitted that he was certifiably crazy about Kelly Morrison. But he couldn't say that, of course. Not to his father. Not even to Kelly. She wasn't ready to hear it.

Would she ever be?

"What are you going to do about it?"

"Be patient, I guess. Hope she'll see how foolish she is to be afraid."

Jared chuckled wryly, sympathetically. "Patience has never been your strong suit."

"No. I'm sure she's aware of that."

"If she knows you well, she is."

Something Kelly said had been haunting him. "She says I have an issue with anger."

For the first time, Jared paused in his work to look at his son. "She thinks *you* have a problem with anger?"

"Yeah. She says I don't know how to express it."

"I see." Jared stroked his chin. "I'm not sure I've ever seen you get really angry. Oh, you've gotten mad plenty of times—but never foaming-at-the-mouth furious."

Shane shrugged. "So I don't have much of a temper. That's a good thing, isn't it?"

"Depends on whether you don't get furious, or whether you feel like you have to repress it, for some reason. I don't get angry all that often, myself, but I don't usually try to hide it when I do."

Shane had seen his father in full temper on only a few

memorable occasions. Jared wasn't loud when he was mad—he got dangerously quiet, in fact—but he was damned intimidating. And he spared no words expressing his displeasure. Cassie, on the other hand, had a fiery temper that matched her red hair. She believed the level of noise she made should express the degree of her anger. Molly had inherited her mother's temper.

Shane got mad sometimes. He simply saw no purpose in wasting time or energy displaying it. He'd been mad as hell at Kelly yesterday—her asinine suggestion that they "postpone" their relationship still made him seethe—but what would have been the point of yelling at her about it?

"I don't know why she's always trying to get me to be mad at someone. You…even herself. It doesn't make sense."

Jared reached for the box of roofing nails. "*Are* you mad at me?"

"No, of course not," Shane answered impatiently. "I told you when we talked about it the other day that I don't blame you for anything in my childhood. Any anger I felt toward you then was irrational, since you were doing the best you could."

"And I told *you* I know I could have done more—and that I wouldn't blame you for being mad about it."

"What would be the point?"

"The point would be getting it off your chest. You let anger build up long enough and it'll eat at you. If you're having trouble letting it out, maybe you should figure out why that is."

"Now you're starting to sound like…" Shane stopped himself just in time.

Jared didn't ask him to fill in the blank.

Shane slanted a look at his father, wondering if Jared

knew more than he was letting on about the identity of the woman they'd been indirectly discussing. "So do you have any advice for me?"

"Every time I've tried to give advice about romance, it's come back to bite me in the butt," Jared drawled.

"You think I should go along with her? Be patient and hope she'll eventually find the nerve to stop hiding her feelings?"

"What else can you do? Other than break it off, of course."

"No." Shane wasn't ready to do that.

"Then you might try something else you've always been very good at."

"What's that?"

Jared smiled. "Charm and persistence. Cassie's always said you'd have made a killing as a salesman if you hadn't wanted to be a rancher."

Shane lifted an eyebrow. "You're suggesting I sell myself to her?"

His father shrugged. "Isn't that what courtship is all about?"

Shane hadn't thought of it quite that way before. "Yeah, I guess it is."

"There you go, then. Now, move down. You're in my way."

Obediently shifting a few feet farther away, Shane thought about his father's words as they continued to work side by side. Charm and persistence, he thought. He didn't know about the former, but he'd always had his share of the latter. Looked like it was time to see if that particular trait paid off when it came to exasperatingly stubborn Kelly Morrison.

Kelly spent Monday at the mall, feverishly shopping for Christmas presents. She was having a hard time getting into the holiday spirit, despite all the decorations and blaring seasonal music, but the outing gave her something to think about other than Shane or her father. She needed that distraction very badly.

When she returned home late that afternoon, she made herself a cup of spiced cider and stacked the gifts she'd purchased on the dining table. She might as well wrap them, she thought, thinking how pretty they would look beneath her tree. Determined to get into the spirit of the holiday, she loaded her CD changer with her three very favorite Christmas CDs—Vince Gill, John Berry and Sawyer Brown—set it on random play and lit a couple of cinnamon-scented candles. And then she pulled out paper and ribbon and tape and bows, humming along with the familiar music as she set to work.

She wished she had her kitten, she mused, thinking how much fun it would be to watch the little white-and-gray fur ball playing with the ribbons and paper. Shane had said it would be ready to leave its mother just after the first of the year. Kelly would enjoy the company.

She had just set the first wrapped gift under the tree when her doorbell rang. Her heart promptly missed a beat. Would she and Shane have another of those painful nonfights? Or would he be ready to talk now, to listen to her reasons for the requests she'd made of him?

But it wasn't Shane at her door. Instead, she found a young woman in a bright red uniform, bearing an enormous arrangement of red-and-white roses mixed with greenery and delicate baby's breath. Kelly gasped. ''Oh, how lovely.''

''Kelly Morrison?'' the young woman asked with a perky smile.

''Yes.''

The woman handed her the flowers. "Enjoy."

She was gone before Kelly could even say, "Thank you."

The sweet scent of roses mingled deliciously with the cinnamon candles as Kelly carried the arrangement to the table. She pulled out the card that had been tucked among the blooms, though she already knew whose name she would find there. But the card didn't bear a name at all. "From your secret admirer," it said instead. "With love."

Of course she knew who had sent the flowers. What she *didn't* know was exactly what the gesture meant. Was this Shane's way of apologizing for the way they'd parted the evening before? Was the cryptic message a signal that he was willing to continue going along with her request to keep their affair a secret? And he'd signed it "With love." Had he used those words only in the generic sense—or should she read more into them than that?

Even when he did something as traditional as sending flowers, Shane could still confuse and unsettle her. Was this the way love was supposed to feel? So uncertain? So complicated? So terrifying?

She would have liked to talk to someone who'd been there. Her fingers almost itched to dial Brynn's number. But what would she say? She couldn't even talk indirectly about her feelings without Brynn wheedling the truth from her. And even though she knew she was being a coward and unfair to Shane, she still couldn't make herself say the words. Entirely too much was at risk, she thought again.

If only she could be more confident about Shane's feelings for her. It had all happened so quickly—almost impulsively. What if he was mistaking affection for something more? What if he'd confused passing infatuation for deeper emotions? Physical attraction for lasting commitment?

She could still remember the startled look in his eyes after their first kiss. In the more than a year that had passed since their first meeting, had he never once until that kiss considered there could be more between them than friendship? Shouldn't that tell them something— that maybe they should think twice about this? That maybe they, like Cameron and Amber, had never been meant to be more than friends?

She closed her eyes and was instantly transported back to that night in his arms. She could feel his lips moving against hers, his hands on her skin, his legs entwined with hers. Just friends? She might have laughed, had she been able to find any humor in the situation. But it seemed to her that she was much more likely to find only heartache.

Joe Walker set up the meeting between Kelly and her father for Thursday at noon. It was Kelly who had insisted on a public meeting place. She didn't know this man, she reminded Joe. She didn't want to try to make conversation with him alone in her apartment.

They selected a popular Southwestern restaurant in west Dallas. They would meet for lunch and conversation, just the two of them. Joe assured Kelly that her father expected nothing from her after that. Just lunch. Kelly thought she could handle that.

"You're sure you're okay doing this alone?" Shane asked her over the telephone Wednesday evening. "You don't need anyone there with you?"

"No. I can handle this. It will be easier since it's to be held in a public place. All I have to do is have lunch with him, ask my questions and then we can part politely at the restaurant door.''

"You make it sound as if you aren't expecting to see him again after tomorrow.''

"It's been sixteen years since our last meeting. I won't hold my breath until the next one.''

"Kelly, do you *want* to do this?'' he asked quietly.

She held the telephone close to her mouth and spoke softly in return. "No. But I think I have to.''

"Are you driving yourself?''

"Yes. I know the area.''

"Is your car running okay?''

"No problem so far. I think you took care of it. Thank you again.''

"I've been told I'm good with my hands.''

Kelly was glad he couldn't see her blush in response to the images that flooded her mind. "I'm sure you have.''

She hadn't seen him since he'd left her apartment Sunday evening. Responsibilities at the ranch were keeping him out of Dallas for now, though he'd called every day. Their conversations had been brief, not particularly satisfying, but he hadn't pressed her about their relationship. He seemed to be giving her the time and space she'd requested—perhaps because he knew how nervous she was about the upcoming meeting with her father. In some ways, she was relieved that she didn't have to deal with her feelings for Shane just now. But deep inside, she missed him much more than she wanted him to stay away.

"I miss you,'' Shane said

She blinked, wondering for a moment if she'd accidentally blurted her thoughts aloud. "I, uh, miss you, too.''

"Well, that's something." His tone was a bit rueful. Without giving her a chance to respond, he added, "I haven't given up on you, Kelly Morrison." He sounded rather amused now—at her, at himself, maybe at both of them. "I'm going to win you with my famous charm and persistence."

"Charm and persistence?" she repeated, smiling despite her qualms.

"Yeah. My dad said those are my—"

"Your dad?" Kelly interrupted with a sudden, suspicious frown. "Shane, did you talk to your father about us? After you promised you wouldn't?"

"I didn't talk to him about us. Well, not exactly."

The faint guilt she heard in his voice only concerned her more. "What do you mean, not exactly?"

"I never used your name. We just talked sort of hypothetically."

Kelly gripped the receiver so hard, her knuckles cracked. She had never underestimated Jared Walker's perceptiveness. She pictured his shrewd eyes trained on her, assessing her as a potential mate for his son, making predictions about what would happen between them— and she shivered in panic. "I wish you hadn't done that."

"I didn't break my word to you. I simply had a brief talk with my father when he asked if there was something bothering me. It was only a passing conversation. Chill out, okay?"

He was probably annoyed with her again, though he would surely deny it if she said so. It happened every time they came close to quarreling. And every time, she worried again that they were making a terrible mistake.

Her silence only seemed to irritate him more. "I've got to go," he said, somewhat abruptly. "I promised

Molly I would keep time for her barrel-race practice. Let me know how it goes with your father, okay?''

Once again, he was withdrawing rather than staying to confront the problem. He had a pattern of retreating when faced with anger—hers or his own. A habit developed when he was twelve years old? How could they understand it if they didn't talk about it? And what would happen if they had a *real* quarrel, after they'd gone public with their feelings? Would Shane run again, leaving her to deal with the consequences in front of all their friends?

This, she thought, was one of the reasons she continued to resist him. Until she completely understood him—until she knew what he kept hidden behind his sexy smiles, she would not risk everything on their tenuous relationship.

''You know, Shane, you keep saying you aren't good at pretending, but you're wrong. You pretend very well that you never get angry. You're pretending right now that you're hanging up only because of a promise you made to Molly, and not because you're mad at me. The difference between us is that I've kept our relationship a secret from everyone else, but I've been honest with you. About my feelings, my fears…and about my anger. I'm angry with you now for talking to your father when you promised you wouldn't.''

''I did *not* tell my father about you. And I'm not mad at you. What is this obsession you have with me being mad at someone?''

''I only want to talk about our feelings.''

''You know, I'm getting a little tired of talking about our feelings. We've been talking, but we aren't getting anywhere. We're still sneaking around acting like nothing's going on, and you're still predicting disaster and refusing to give me any indication of when—or if—we can date openly.''

"I said after the holidays,'' she answered defensively. Then added, "Maybe.''

"'Maybe,''' he parroted. "But in the meantime, I'm supposed to see you at the family Christmas gatherings and act like you're nothing more to me than a friend. A pal. A cousin. Do you really think I can pull that off?''

"I hoped we could. It just seems so much easier.''

"No one ever said this would be easy. But I'd like to think what we've found is worth the effort.''

She swallowed painfully. "Shane…''

"I've got to go. Molly's waiting for me. We'll talk again tomorrow. Good luck with your meeting with your father.''

A moment later there was a dial tone in her ear. Kelly stared at the receiver for a moment, then thumped it against her head. How had she ever gotten herself into this situation?

Shane and Jared leaned against a wooden fence that surrounded the practice arena Jared had built for Molly's use. While Molly put her horse through its paces within the arena, her father and brother watched closely, occasionally calling out advice, neither taking their eyes from the slender redhead on the well-trained mare. Shane looked away only occasionally to check the stopwatch he gripped in his right hand.

As intently as Jared watched his daughter, he proved that he was equally aware of his son when he asked, "How's it going with the girlfriend?''

Shane snorted. "It isn't.''

"She's still dragging her heels?''

"Yeah.''

"Did you have a quarrel with her?"

"No, not really."

"Oh. You sounded sort of mad. I thought you'd had a fight."

"I'm *not* mad," Shane snapped, wishing everyone would quit trying to make him admit an anger he didn't want to feel. And then almost immediately he regretted his sharp tone. "Sorry. I'm just...stressed."

"You don't owe me an apology."

"I shouldn't have snarled at you. It isn't your fault I'm having problems with a woman."

Molly showed her horse to a walk, and Jared turned to Shane. "You know, it's okay if you..."

"Shane!" Cassie called out from her house behind them. "The garbage disposal is broken again. Can you look at it?"

"I'll be right there." He handed the stopwatch to Jared. "Don't worry about me, Dad. I'll handle all this somehow. Now I'd better go fix that garbage disposal before Cassie gets impatient."

He was aware that his father watched him as he walked toward the house, but he wasn't sure what exactly was going on behind Jared's inscrutable expression.

Chapter Fourteen

Kelly was so nervous when she entered the restaurant the next day that her stomach was in knots. She couldn't imagine that she would be able to eat a bite. She wondered now why she had insisted on a lunch meeting. She'd thought the routines of mealtime would ease the awkwardness of this reunion, but now she worried that it would only make it worse.

She should have had him come to her apartment, she fretted. Or maybe they should have met at the offices of D'Alessandro Investigations.

Or maybe they shouldn't have met at all.

"May I help you?" an attractive hostess inquired when Kelly paused in the restaurant lobby.

"I'm meeting someone here. The name is Morrison."

The hostess checked a list, then nodded and signaled to one of her co-workers. "Your party is already seated. Marie will escort you to your table."

"Thank you." Taking a deep, steadying breath, Kelly followed the plump, smiling Marie into the lunch-crowded dining room.

A dignified-looking man in a dark blue uniform stood as Kelly approached his table. His sandy hair, graying at the temples, was cut short, and sun lines were etched around the corners of his dark green eyes, but he was still a striking-looking man. He was only a year or two over fifty, Kelly realized with a start. Her mother would have been fifty-one this year, had she lived. She'd just turned forty when she died.

The thought of her mother's lonely and untimely death made her expression cool when she greeted her father. "Hello." She had called him "Daddy" when she'd seen him last. That affectionate term seemed inappropriate now.

"Kelly." He looked as uncomfortable as she felt. His movements were a bit stiff when he took a step toward her. "It's good to see you."

She moved quickly toward her chair, in case he felt it necessary to hug her. "I have to admit I was surprised to hear from you," she said as she took her seat.

"I'm sure you were." Colonel Jack Morrison sat across the table from her, his eyes trained on her face. "You've grown into a beautiful young woman, Kelly. You look very much like your mother."

Kelly's memories of her mother were of a woman ravaged by pain and disease, her hair gone, her skin pale and dry. "I'll have to take your word for that."

Jack looked grim, but seemed determined to keep the conversation going. "I noticed you were limping a bit when you joined me. Have you injured yourself?"

"I was in a serious car accident more than a year ago.

The limp is what remains after two operations and six weeks of hospitalization.''

Her father grimaced. "I'm sorry. I didn't know."

"No. You wouldn't, would you?"

A waiter approached the table. "May I bring you something to drink?"

"I'll have a margarita. Kelly?"

"Just water, please."

The waiter nodded toward their untouched menus. "I'll be back soon with your drinks. I'll take your orders when you're ready."

When they were alone again, Jack made an ineffectual motion with his hands. "Are you still in any pain from your injuries?"

"No." She saw no need to mention the discomfort she felt after overexertion, or when the weather turned cold and damp.

"That's good. So...you're a college student?"

"A graduate student. I'll have my masters degree soon."

"What's your major?"

"Communication disorders."

He nodded. "Sounds like a good field to get into. I'd imagine there's a demand for good therapists."

"I enjoy it."

An awkward silence followed. Their drinks arrived and Jack took a sip of his margarita, waving the waiter away. "We'll let you know when we're ready to order."

"Take your time, sir."

Jack set his drink on the table and rested his elbows on either side of it. His eyes focused on Kelly's face. "Okay, let's have it. I expect you've got a few things you'd like to say to me."

She sipped her water, grateful that her hand was

steady when she set the glass down. "You called this meeting. I assumed *you* were the one with something to say."

"You're not going to make this easy for me, are you?"

She didn't smile in response to his wry tone. "Why should I?"

"I'll resist saying 'because I'm your father'"

Kelly's finger tightened on the water glass. "Good call."

He sighed. "I know you're angry with me, and you have every reason to be. I haven't been a father to you, Kelly."

"No. I was orphaned nearly eleven years ago, when my mother died after a long, terrible illness."

"I talked to your mother several times when she was ill. She assured me you were being raised in a good home, by a nice family."

Kelly was startled. She hadn't known her parents had spoken after her mother became ill. "I was placed in a foster home. It wasn't a family. There was a good-hearted, but rather strict, widow who took in foster children like boarders to supplement her income. She was good to me. I was well fed, well-groomed, and well cared for. But I had no family."

Jack looked somberly down at his hands. "That isn't what I was led to believe about your situation. Your mother implied that you had practically been adopted by a loving family."

Kelly suspected that it had been her mother's pride that had compelled her to embellish Kelly's circumstances. She would not have wanted her ex-husband to think she hadn't provided well for the child she'd been forced to raise alone. "So because you thought I'd been taken in by another family, you saw no need to contact me in any way? Not for any of my birthdays or Christmases or graduations? Not even when my mother died?''

''I have no excuse for my absence from your life,'' Jack answered flatly. ''I was never cut out to be a father. I tried to tell Greta that, but she never understood. She was miserable in Germany, desperate to come to this country. I was her ticket here. Our marriage didn't last long, but I thought I'd given her what she wanted—a home in the U.S. A child.''

''And what did *you* want?''

''My career. It's all that ever really mattered to me.''

At least she couldn't accuse him of not being honest with her. ''Why did you want to meet with me today?''

''Two reasons. I wanted to make sure for myself that you're okay. And I promised my fiancée that I would meet with you.''

''Your fiancée?'' Kelly repeated weakly.

''Her name is Evelyn Dobson. She works for the American Embassy in Italy. We're getting married next month.''

''Congratulations,'' she said dryly. ''Why did your fiancée want you to meet with me?''

''When I told her I have a daughter I haven't seen in sixteen years, she said she didn't want to begin our marriage with that uncertainty hanging over us. She thought it best if I found out where you were living and how you were getting along. Whether you needed anything from me.''

''In other words, she didn't want me showing up out of the blue to make demands on you, right?''

''That's one way of putting it, I guess.'' Jack seemed to accept that Kelly didn't want any sugarcoated answers. ''She's never had any children of her own. She's forty-five and isn't prepared to fill the role of step-mother—or stepgrandmother.''

"She needn't worry about either possibility," Kelly assured him coolly. "I'm not interested in having a step-mother at this point. I have no children, but if I ever do, I will be prepared to provide for them myself—just as my mother did for me. I have a career, a home, friends and a close, honorary family here in Dallas. I've gotten along very well without you so far, Colonel, and you can assure your fiancée that I will continue to do so.''

"This isn't the way I'd hoped our reunion would go." There was genuine regret in his voice.

"You mean you didn't want honesty? You wanted me to throw myself in your arms and tell you I forgive you for deserting me? You wanted to pat me on the head the way you did when I was eight, and then leave me hoping you'll contact me again someday? You were hoping you wouldn't have to tell me the truth about why you initiated this meeting?''

"I'm not sure what I wanted," Jack replied. "But this wasn't it.''

"Forgive me if I gave up on my fantasies about you at my mother's funeral." She had no intention of telling him about the futile hopes she'd clung to until her high school graduation.

"I'm sorry, Kelly. You deserved better.''

"Yes," she answered quietly. "I did. And I'm very angry with you for denying me the childhood I dreamed about when I was a lonely little girl. But if it makes you feel any better, I don't hate you. I can let the anger go. I wish you the best in your marriage and hope you're very happy. I won't be asking you for anything in the future, or anticipating anything more than I've ever gotten from you.''

"Under the circumstances, I suppose that's more than I should have expected from you."

She studied him across the table. "Look at it this way—were you really prepared to be a father at this point? Would you have hired someone to find me if your fiancée hadn't asked you to?"

He hesitated long enough that she had her answer. "That's what I thought," she said.

He searched her face with a thoughtful expression. "If it matters to you—I'm very proud of you. You've succeeded against very stiff odds, and with very little help from anyone apparently. That took a lot of courage, a great deal of determination. I'd like to think you got some of that drive from me."

"I think most of it came from my mother," she countered frankly. "She was a very strong and self-sufficient woman."

"Yes, she was."

"Will you answer one question for me?"

He nodded. "Of course."

"Did you ever love my mother?"

"In my own way," he answered wryly. "Just as I love you, though not the way I'm sure you would choose to be loved by your father."

"And Evelyn? Do you love her?"

There was a pause before he answered. "Evelyn and I are well suited. We expect to spend our retirement years very comfortably together."

He smiled crookedly at the look on her face. "That arrangement must sound very cold and bland to someone your age. But it suits us."

Kelly wondered if Jack Morrison was capable of really loving anyone. And she wondered how much she had inherited from him besides his eyes. "Then I wish you well."

"Thank you." He picked up his menu. "Shall we order?"

Kelly glanced at the menu in front of her. She couldn't imagine eating anything now. "Would you mind terribly if I don't stay for lunch? There are several things I need to do, and I think you and I have said all we need to say."

Jack closed his menu and set it aside, his expression resigned. "Before you go, there's something I want to give you. Call it a Christmas present."

"Another bicycle?" she couldn't resist asking.

Giving her a faintly chiding look, he reached into his pocket and pulled out a small, Christmas-wrapped box. He set it on the table in front of her. "Open it."

Hesitantly she picked up the box and slipped off the ribbon. Her fingers felt unusually clumsy as she peeled away the paper. Her breath caught when she saw the hinged, gold oval nestled on the cotton inside the small box.

"Look inside," her father urged.

Very slowly, she opened the locket. There were two photographs inside. One depicted a young couple, the man in uniform, the woman in traditional German dress, her hair in braids around her head. She was smiling, Kelly noted with a lump in her throat. She looked happy. The second photograph was of a baby girl, chubby and laughing, dressed in foaming lace. She, too, looked happy.

"Your mother gave me that when we decided to split up. I've carried it with me ever since. I thought you might like to have it."

For the first time since she had arrived, Kelly found

herself on the verge of tears. "Thank you," she murmured.

Her father's smile was tinged with sadness. "You can show it to those kids you'll probably have someday."

She nodded, and reached for her purse. "Goodbye, Daddy." She added the term deliberately this time, bidding farewell as much to the dream as to the man.

"Goodbye, Katarina," he replied, using the name her mother had always called her. "Take care of yourself."

"I always have," she said, and then turned and walked away without looking back.

She didn't cry until she was at home in her apartment, the locket open in her hands. Only then did she acknowledge to herself that she'd had a secret hope that her father would have a very good reason for staying out of her life for so long. That he would convince her that he deeply regretted missing those years with her. Maybe she'd had a childish fantasy that he wanted to be a father to her now, that she would finally have a family of her own.

Once again her father had disappointed her. She allowed herself to shed a few tears in reaction, and then she dried her eyes and put the locket away.

She had things to do, she told herself. A life to get on with. She didn't need her father; she didn't need anyone, really.

She had learned long ago not to expect too much when it came to her personal relationships. It was a lesson she wouldn't forget again.

It was Friday, the week before Christmas, and Shane had never been in less of a holiday mood. It was all he could do to socialize nicely with his family and with

Brynn and Joe D'Alessandro, who had joined them for dinner.

Molly had a school assignment during the holidays to do an in-depth interview of someone other than her parents who had a career she found interesting. She and Shane had discussed the careers available to her within her extended family—accounting, advertising, charity administration, private investigation and real-estate sales. She had expressed an interest in Joe's orthopedic surgery, and Joe had graciously agreed to answer as many questions as she wanted to ask. Cassie had said the least she could do was prepare a nice meal as repayment, and since everyone knew how much Cassie enjoyed entertaining, the evening had evolved from there.

Shane, Jared, Cassie and Brynn moved to the den to visit while Molly questioned her cousin's husband at the dinning room table after dinner. "I warn you," Cassie said to Brynn, "This might take a while. Molly's been doing her research. She has a long list of questions about bone screws and joint replacement and vertebra fusing and heavens knows what else."

Brynn smiled. "I'm sure Joe is loving every minute of it. He loves to talk about his work."

Cassie glanced at her watch. "We'll rescue him in an hour. I think that's long enough."

"Are you all going to Michelle and Tony's house tomorrow evening for Katie's birthday party?" Brynn asked.

"Of course we'll be there," Cassie answered on behalf of her family.

Jared sighed. "There sure are a lot of parties this time of year."

Shane chuckled. "In this family, there are a lot of parties at any time of year."

"I happen to like that," Cassie said. "Especially at this time of year when things are slow enough here at the ranch for you and your father to have time to attend most of the gatherings."

"Michelle said Katie's really looking forward to her party," Brynn commented. "It's easy to feel overlooked, I suppose, when one's birthday is so very close to Christmas."

"Katie's never been the type to be overlooked for long," Jared drawled, making everyone laugh as they thought of the little girl whose song Shane had once declared should be, "I'm Gonna to Make You Love Me."

"Is Kelly going to be there tomorrow?" Shane asked Brynn, keeping his tone as nonchalant as possible. He thought he felt his father glance his way, and he wondered again if Jared had guessed the identity of Shane's secret lover.

Although *lover* wasn't exactly an accurate term, he thought glumly. He hadn't even seen Kelly since last weekend. They'd talked on the phone, but she'd always seemed to be in a hurry, claiming other obligations. They'd barely talked about her meeting with her father yesterday. All he knew was that she hadn't found the meeting particularly satisfying and didn't expect to see her father again any time soon.

He had wanted Kelly to join them for dinner this evening, but she'd made plans to do something with Amber. Amber needed her friends now, she had added somberly. A broken heart was difficult to handle alone. He had been left to wonder in frustration if Kelly had started to compare their relationship to Cameron and Amber's again. Every time she did that she pulled back again. He didn't know what it was going to take for him to convince her to give them a fair chance.

"Kelly can't come to the birthday party. She has other plans."

There was such smug satisfaction in Brynn's announcement that Shane's eyes narrowed in suspicion. "Oh?" he asked, ultracasually. "What other plans?"

Practically patting herself on the back, Brynn replied, "The hospital administrator is hosting an annual holiday reception tomorrow evening for all the staff members who've joined the team during the past year. I found out that Steve Carter didn't have a date, so I suggested he call Kelly. Then I called her and ordered her to accept. She was a little shy about it, but I reminded her that he's a very nice guy who's a little shy himself. I think the two of them will get along very well."

Shane realized that his hands had clenched into fists. He loosened them deliberately. He hoped his voice sounded more normal to the others than it did to him when he asked, "When was this arranged?"

"She told him yesterday that she would go with him. It was after her awkward meeting with her father. I was spending the evening with her, letting her talk out her feelings about the reunion with her father, when Steve called. She started to make excuses, but I convinced her to accept. Okay, I nagged her," Brynn added sheepishly. "But I thought it would be good for her."

Shane pushed himself abruptly to his feet. "I hope she has a great time. Now, if you'll excuse me, I have to feed the horses."

"That can wait, can't it?" Cassie asked, looking surprised by his behavior.

"I really need to check on Runaway. He seemed to

be wheezing earlier. I don't want him coming down with a respiratory infection.''

''So that's why you've been so distracted this evening.'' Cassie nodded as if in sudden enlightenment. ''You and that horse of yours. Sometimes I think you have a psychic connection with him.''

''Who says I don't?'' Shane retorted, forcing a smile.

Aware that everyone was watching him—especially his father—Shane kept that smile on his face until he left the room. And then he allowed it to be replaced by the tremendous scowl that had been building inside him.

It was all he could do not to start throwing things in the barn. He had a childish impulse to kick something, preferably a doctor named Steve Carter. Even as that ignoble urge crossed his mind, he knew it was unfair. He could blame Carter or he could blame Brynn, but Kelly was the one he was really mad at.

How could she go on a date with another man now, no matter how determinedly Brynn had pushed her about it? Why couldn't she just have told the truth, damn it, and said she wasn't free to date anyone else?

He slammed the lid of the grain bin, making the horses in their stalls start in alarm.

''Take it easy, Shane. I just replaced those hinges.''

He turned slowly to face his father. ''I've taken care of everything out here. You can go back to your guests.''

''Molly and Joe are still involved in their interview and Cassie and Brynn are having a gossip session in the den. I thought maybe you'd want to talk.''

Shane reached for a broom and began to sweep up some grain he'd spilled through angry carelessness. ''About what?''

''About Kelly going on a date with another man tomorrow night.''

Shane's hands white-knuckled around the broom. "Why should I care about that?"

Jared's tone was patient. "If you don't want to talk about it, say so, but don't treat me like I'm stupid."

He sighed. "I know you're not stupid, Dad. Sorry."

"So, do you want to talk?"

He hesitated only a moment. He hadn't really broken his promise, he rationalized. Jared had guessed the truth. Besides, Kelly was the one who'd accepted a date with another guy.

"She still won't give us a fair chance," he blurted in frustration. "Just because we have a family connection, she's afraid it will ruin everything if we start dating. She thinks if something goes wrong—and she's convinced it will—she'll lose her friendship with the family. She said it's inevitable that she'd be the one pushed out because I belong in the family and she doesn't. She said it will be too awkward for everyone if she stays, and then she'll be all alone. I keep trying to tell her how ridiculous that is. This family's crazy about her. Even if she and I have problems—and I'm not so sure that's going to happen— it won't change the way anyone feels about Kelly."

Jared leaned back against a support beam, his arms crossed over his chest. "You really don't understand why she's worried?"

"Not entirely. It just seems so unreasonable."

Rubbing the back of his neck with one hand, Jared shook his head. "You remember when you were a teenager, after you came to live with me, those times when I would make you mad? You know, times when you wanted to stay out past curfew, or when I made you come inside to do your homework when you wanted to ride your horse?"

Though Shane didn't know what that had to do with

this conversation, he nodded. "I got annoyed at times, but all teenagers do, I guess."

"You never lost your temper. You never let me see how mad you were. You just swallowed whatever you wanted to say and did whatever I asked."

"You're complaining about that? Wasn't that what you wanted from me?"

"What I wanted was for you to trust me enough to know that I wouldn't stop loving you if you lost your temper. I might have yelled at you or grounded you or whatever I thought was appropriate, but I would never have stopped loving you. I would never have sent you away."

"I know that."

"Did you know it then? After all those years with your mother, when I wasn't there for you, did you really trust me to be on your side even if you misbehaved?"

Shane frowned. *Had* he been afraid his father would stop loving him if he caused any trouble? Several of their relatives had expressed surprise that he was such an obedient, good-natured teenager, especially after his difficult childhood, but he had deliberately chosen to follow the rules. Living with his father had been a dream that had sustained him during the first twelve years of his life. He had never taken that good fortune for granted, had never risked screwing it up.

"Maybe it took me a while to feel completely secure after we got together," he admitted slowly. "But deep inside, I knew you would never send me back."

"You found that security because I'm your father. Because we're family. You knew that nothing you could do, no matter what, could make me push you away."

"Yeah, I guess I figured that out pretty quickly."

Jared nodded. "Kelly doesn't have that reassurance.

Her father never cared enough about her to even visit her when she was a kid. The extended family she's found for herself since—Brynn, the Walkers, the D'Alessandros—none of them are really related to her. She doesn't have the bonds of blood and history that you have. She really is on her own if her ties to us are broken.''

"But…"

"As for whether she should have confidence in you… Have you ever told her exactly how you feel about her?"

"She won't let me," Shane said defensively.

"Maybe you haven't tried hard enough. Maybe you're a little afraid yourself."

Shane winced.

"You said she's asked you several times why you won't show your anger," Jared continued. "Maybe it isn't just your anger she's afraid you're hiding from her. Maybe she feels like you're keeping too much of yourself hidden from her. Maybe she's afraid that if you can't even tell her when you're annoyed with her, there's a chance you won't be able to share your other feelings with her, either."

Moving very slowly, Shane set the broom back in its place. "I haven't looked at it that way. You think when she pushes me to talk about my anger, she really wants me to talk about *everything* I feel?"

"Women like to have things spelled out," Jared explained with a slight smile. "You should have heard Cassie urging me to be more open about my emotions when she and I were just getting together. It wasn't something I was particularly comfortable with, and it's still not always easy for me to express what I'm feeling. But it was something she needed from me, and I tried to accommodate her. And I found out that it's better to get everything out in the open.''

Shane rubbed his chin. "So it would be a good thing for me to tell you I was really mad that you spent so much time on a ship when I was a kid?''

Jared's eyebrows rose. "If that's what you feel, you have every right to say so.''

"And you remember that time I wanted to stay out all night after the high school homecoming game and you made me be home by 1:00 a.m.? That really torqued me off.''

"I see. Well…''

"And when I wanted to spend a summer hitchhiking across country with Scott, and you told me you'd lock me in a closet first, I—''

"Okay, you've made your point," Jared cut in. "But watch your mouth. I can still send you to your room.''

And he would probably go, Shane thought with wry amusement. But he would know even then that his father still loved him. "It's cool, Dad. I got over it.''

"I'm glad to hear that. Now, what are you going to do about Kelly?''

He drew a deep breath. "I don't know yet.''

What he *wanted* to do was to forbid her to go on that date. But something told him that would be a mistake— even if he could get away with it. What he had to do, instead, was let her come back to him. But first, perhaps he should tell her exactly how he felt.

Jared rested a hand on his shoulder. "You'll figure it out, son. I have faith in you.''

"How long have you known I'm in love with Kelly?'' Shane asked, studying his father's face.

"How long has it been since you met her?''

"Just over a year and a half.''

Jared nodded. ''That's how long I've known.''

Frowning, Shane shook his head. ''You couldn't have. I didn't know it myself, until just before Thanksgiving, just a few weeks ago. Before that, Kelly and I thought we were just friends.''

''That's what you've been telling yourselves.'' Jared sounded vaguely amused.

Grimacing, Shane asked warily, ''Does anyone else know?''

''I don't think so.''

''Cassie?''

''Not as far as I'm aware. She and I haven't talked about it.''

''Then how did you...?''

''I'm your father.''

Jared seemed to think that was explanation enough. And maybe, for them, it was.

''We'd better get back inside to our guests,'' Jared said, stepping toward the door. ''You coming?''

''Yeah. I'll be there in a minute.''

''You know where to find me if you need anything.''

''Thanks, Dad.''

Alone again with the horses, Shane leaned his elbow on a wooden gate and looked into a stall. ''Well, Runaway? Any suggestions?''

The horse snorted into his feed trough.

''Yeah,'' Shane said with little humor. ''That's pretty much what *I* thought.''

Chapter Fifteen

Kelly was sitting at her dressing room table, staring blindly into her mirror, when the telephone rang, jarring her into motion. She jumped up to grab the phone, hoping it would be Steve Carter, telling her he'd had a medical emergency and would be forced to cancel their date.

She'd been an idiot to agree to this in the first place. But he'd called when she'd still been reeling from her meeting with her father and Brynn had been so insistent. Kelly hadn't been able to come up with a good reason to refuse, short of the truth. And now she was committed to a date she didn't want to go on, involved in a deception that was weighing so heavily on her, she could hardly breathe. "Hello?"

"I just wanted to tell you I hope you have a good time on your date."

Her mouth suddenly went dry, her knees weak. She sank to the edge of the bed. "Shane."

"It occurred to me that this could be your way of trying to *really* make me mad. You've seemed to want me to lose my temper."

"No." She was appalled that he could think that was the primary reason for this outing—to spur Shane into finally, completely opening up with her. That was ridiculous—wasn't it? "I got into this as a favor to Brynn. I didn't know how to refuse without...without..."

"Without telling her the truth? That you and I are together now and that you aren't interested in going out with other men? Or *is* that the truth?"

"Shane, don't..."

"I hope it doesn't disappoint you if I tell you I'm not really mad. And, no, I'm not repressing my anger or pretending to be cool when I'm not, or anything like that. I hate it that you're spending the evening with another guy. I mean, I *really* hate it, but I sort of understand why you're doing it. You're scared. You're confused. And maybe I haven't done enough to reassure you that everything's going to be okay."

She blinked. "I don't..."

"Like an idiot, I've expected you to know without me telling you that this isn't a passing fling for me. Maybe I thought you could read my mind and understand that I didn't think there would be a problem with my family because I didn't believe there would ever be a serious problem between *us*. I had no intention of ever letting you go once I convinced you we belonged together."

A sizable lump had formed in Kelly's throat during Shane's quiet speech. She tried to speak around it. "I didn't know..."

"Of course you didn't know. I didn't tell you, did I? Maybe I thought you understood—or maybe I was a coward, too afraid of rejection to risk revealing my feelings. But, just so you have no lingering doubts, I love you, Kelly. I think I have for a very long time, maybe since the first time we met.''

Her heart convulsed. Of all the things she had thought Shane might say when she'd recognized his voice on the phone, this wasn't one of them. *He loved her?* Why was he telling her this now? It wasn't something he would say just because she was about to leave on a date with another man, was it? Surely he didn't think her date with Steve was a ploy to make Shane jealous, or anything so shallow and stupid.

Yet…was it possible that he really meant it? ''Shane, I…''

He didn't seem to expect a reply from her at the moment. ''If you want me to keep it a secret until I've convinced you of my feelings, I will. I'll bite my tongue until it bleeds if I have to, but no one will know until you're ready—except my father, who has already guessed. It won't be easy, because what I really want to do is yell to the world that I am hat-over-boots in love with beautiful, sexy, smart Kelly Morrison—but you can trust me to keep it secret until you have faith in me, even if it takes the rest of my life to prove it to you.''

Tears were rolling down her face now, ruining the makeup she had applied so carefully for this date she didn't want. ''Shane…''

''Think about what I said while you're out with that guy tonight, okay? And call me if you want to give it another try. I love you, Kelly.''

He hung up before she could whisper his name again.

Kelly had a completely miserable evening. She tried her best to hide it; to do otherwise would have been unforgivably rude to Dr. Steve Carter, who was making a real effort to entertain her. But his jokes weren't as funny as Shane's, and he didn't quite understand her feeble attempts at humor. He didn't like the music, books or movies she liked. He seemed to enjoy the staid, formal hospital reception, while Kelly found it terribly dull.

All in all, it wasn't a very successful first date. And Kelly was well aware that the main reason she had such a lousy time was because she wasn't with Shane. Shane, who had said he loved her. Shane, whom she loved so desperately in return.

It was still early when the reception ended. Steve and Kelly left the room arm in arm, probably looking like a very nice couple. Kelly felt like such a fraud. But it was immediately apparent that all her efforts to pretend to enjoy herself hadn't fooled her companion.

"I was going to suggest we go out for drinks or something after the reception, but I think you'd rather I take you home now," he said when they were in his car again.

She looked at him in guilt-stricken apology. "I'm sorry, Steve. I hope I haven't hurt your feelings. It's just…tonight is not a good time for me."

"You're in love with someone else, right?"

Kelly stared at him, stunned to hear those words from a near stranger.

He gave a rueful shrug. "Trust me, I know the look. It's sort of the story of my life."

"I'm sorry," she repeated. "I'm sure I would have had a very nice time tonight, if I hadn't been so distracted with a personal problem. It would have been more fair to you if I'd made an excuse not to come."

He smiled wryly and started the car. "I have a feeling

your friend Brynn had a lot to do with that. She can be quite...persuasive.''

"Don't tell me she pressured you into this, too," Kelly said with a groan and a blush of embarrassment.

"I wasn't exactly an unwilling participant. I enjoyed visiting with you at the charity dance. I thought we could have a nice evening."

Her guilt immediately doubled. ''I'm sorry to have disappointed you.''

The smile he gave her was quite charming, though it didn't have at all the same effect on her that Shane's sexy, dimpled grins always had. "You didn't disappoint me at all," he assured her.

He really was a very nice guy, even if there was no chance she would ever see him—or any other man besides Shane—as more than a friend. She studied him as they drove out of the parking lot, thinking of someone who could appreciate him much more. "Did Heather Pearson give you her telephone number, by any chance?"

"Heather...?" He nodded in remembrance. "Oh, yes. The brunette who asked me to dance with her at the charity thing. I think she did give me her number. I probably still have it somewhere. But, to be honest, I thought she was a little...well, flaky.''

Kelly laughed softly. "She is actually. But in the very nicest way. She's one of my closest friends. I think you might like her, if you got to know her a little better.''

He seemed intrigued. ''You think so?''

''I really do. She's a lot of fun.''

Steve looked suddenly cautious. ''Is there any chance she's in love with someone else?''

''None,'' Kelly assured him confidently. Heather had made no secret to her friends about how much she wished to find someone special. Maybe Steve Carter would be that special someone.

"Maybe I'll call her sometime."

"Maybe you should."

He chuckled. "This has turned out to be a most unexpected evening."

"I know. And now I'm going to make another request. Instead of taking me home, would you mind dropping me off at a friend's house? There's a family birthday party I'd like to drop in on—and it's actually closer to here than my apartment anyway."

"How will you get home afterward?"

"I'll find a ride." She knew exactly who she wanted to take her home.

He agreed very graciously, merely asking for directions. And Kelly felt a thrill of anticipation mingle with the guilt she still felt about the unsuccessful date with the man who wasn't Shane Walker.

Tony answered the door when Kelly rang his doorbell. He looked startled, but pleased to see her. "Kelly. This is a nice surprise. I thought you wouldn't be able to make it tonight."

"I got away early. Is, er, everyone still here?"

"Of course. The kids are all upstairs, playing with Katie's new toys. The adults are in the den. They'll be delighted to see you."

He escorted her to the door of the den, where she paused to make a quick survey of the room. At a glance, she identified five Walker siblings and their spouses—all present except for Lindsay and Nick, who wouldn't be back in the state until Christmas. A few of the cousins were also in the room—the three Samples siblings, Brynn and Joe—and Shane, who was sitting on one of several couches in the big room, engaged in a spirited conversation with his uncle Ryan while Molly hung over the back of the couch, listening to every word. Everyone seemed to be talking and laughing and having a wonderful time—quite a contrast to the quiet reception she had attended earlier.

She would so much rather be here.

Shane didn't notice her at first, since his back was partially turned to her. Jared, standing across the room with his wife, was the first to spot Kelly standing there in the doorway. His eyes narrowed on her face, and then he smiled. Her cheeks warming a little, Kelly smiled shyly back at him, hoping what she read in his handsomely weathered face was approval.

"Hey, everyone. Look who's been able to join us, after all," Tony called out from behind her.

Everyone automatically looked their way. Kelly heard her name called out from several directions, and heard Brynn ask in exasperation what she was doing there. But, ignoring the others for the moment, Kelly's eyes were locked with Shane's as he turned on the couch to look at her.

Something thumped at her feet.

"Uh—Kelly, you dropped your purse," Tony murmured, bending from behind her to retrieve it.

She couldn't seem to move to reach for it.

Very slowly, Shane rose to his feet, his gaze still holding hers. Without glancing away from her, or responding to anything being said to either of them, he crossed the room, his steps deliberate, his cowboy-lean body moving with the rolling gait and innate grace that had always made her throat tighten in appreciation, even when she wouldn't admit it. It tightened again now.

He stopped only an inch or so away from her. She stared up at him, letting her surrender show in her face.

Either the room fell quiet around them, or Kelly simply tuned out everyone except Shane.

"How was your date?" he asked, his voice low and gravelly.

"Miserable," she answered simply. "And, Shane—I don't care who knows why."

His adorable, "evil-child grin" flashed across his face. "Good. Because I think I'm about to blow our secret."

And then he reached out and pulled her into his arms, completely oblivious to anyone around them.

She thought she heard someone gasp when his mouth covered hers. Several exclamations of surprise. And someone—Molly, she thought—saying, "All right, Shane!"

Kelly discovered that she simply didn't care. She was tired of pretending she wasn't deeply, totally, irrevocably in love with Shane Walker.

Her arms were around his neck, and his were locked behind her back when he lifted his head. "I love you," he murmured.

"I love you, too," she replied with a misty smile.

"You won't ever have to feel like an outsider in this family again," he assured her. "Once we're married, there'll be no further question about who really belongs and who doesn't."

Her legs went weak. She clung to him more tightly. "Uh—married?"

"Married," he repeated firmly. "That's what we do in this family when we find the one we want to spend the rest of our life with."

The rest of their lives. Shane wasn't the type to make such a commitment lightly, Kelly realized in wonder.

And neither was she.

"What on earth is going on here?" Brynn demanded, standing close by with her fists planted on her hips. "Shane, did I just hear you ask Kelly to *marry* you?"

Still holding Kelly in his arms, Shane grinned at his cousin. "Yep."

Obviously stunned, Brynn looked at Kelly. "And did you accept?"

Kelly smiled at her best friend—the sister of her heart—and then turned her eyes back up to Shane. "Yes."

He kissed her again as the room burst into pandemonium around them. Kelly and Shane were suddenly surrounded by family, everyone congratulating them, showering them with questions, expressing surprise, delight, and complete acceptance of this wonderful new development.

And Kelly knew then that she would never feel like an outsider again.

* * * * *

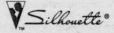

If you enjoyed what you just read,
then we've got an offer you can't resist!

Take 2 bestselling
love stories FREE!
Plus get a FREE surprise gift!

No one can anticipate the unexpected,
be it lust, love or larceny...

SOMETHING TO HIDE

Two exciting
full-length novels by

TESS
GERRITSEN

and

LYNN
ERICKSON

Intrigue and romance are combined in
this thrilling collection of heart-stopping
adventure with a guaranteed happy ending.

Available October 1999 at your favorite retail outlet.

HARLEQUIN®
Makes any time special ™

Visit us at www.romance.net

PSBR21099

Silhouette ® SPECIAL EDITION ®

LINDSAY McKENNA

**delivers two more exciting books in her
heart-stopping new series:**

**MORGAN'S MERCENARIES
III
THE HUNTERS**

Coming in July 1999:
HUNTER'S WOMAN
Special Edition #1255

Ty Hunter wanted his woman back from the moment he set his
piercing gaze on her. For despite the protest on Dr. Catt Alborak's
soft lips, Ty was on a mission to give the stubborn beauty
everything he'd foolishly denied her once—his heart,
his soul—and most of all, his child....

And coming in October 1999:
HUNTER'S PRIDE
Special Edition #1274

Devlin Hunter had a way with the ladies, but when it came to his
job as a mercenary, the brooding bachelor worked alone. Until
his latest assignment paired him up with Kulani Dawson, a feisty
beauty whose tender vulnerabilities brought out his every
protective instinct—and chipped away at his proud vow to never
fall in love....

Look for the exciting series finale in early 2000—when
MORGAN'S MERCENARIES: THE HUNTERS comes to
Silhouette Desire®!

Available at your favorite retail outlet.

Silhouette ®

Coming this September 1999
from SILHOUETTE BOOKS
and bestselling author

RACHEL LEE

CONARD
COUNTY:
Boots &
Badges

Alicia Dreyfus—a desperate woman on the run—
is about to discover that she *can* come home
again...to Conard County. Along the way she
meets the man of her dreams—and brings together
three other couples, whose love blossoms beneath
the bold Wyoming sky.

Enjoy four complete, **brand-new** stories in one
extraordinary volume.

Available at your favorite retail outlet.

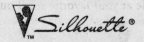

THE FORTUNES OF TEXAS

*Membership in this family has its privileges
…and its price.
But what a fortune can't buy,
a true-bred Texas love is sure to bring!*

Coming in October 1999…

The Baby Pursuit

by

LAURIE PAIGE

When the newest Fortune heir was kidnapped, the prominent family turned to Devin Kincaid to find the missing baby. The dedicated FBI agent never expected his investigation might lead him to the altar with society princess Vanessa Fortune….

THE FORTUNES OF TEXAS continues with **Expecting… In Texas** by **Marie Ferrarella**, available in November 1999 from Silhouette Books.

Available at your favorite retail outlet.

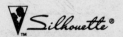

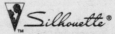